I0694320

THE MALFUNCTION

Also by Orval Wax

The Deilonium Trilogy

The Malfunction, Book 1 of *The Deilonium Trilogy*
Robots and Renegades, Book 2 of *The Deilonium Trilogy*
Operation War Whoop, Book 3 of *The Deilonium Trilogy*

THE MALFUNCTION

BOOK 1 OF THE DEILONIUM TRILOGY

ORVAL WAX

THE MALFUNCTION
Book 1 of The Deilonium Trilogy

Copyright © 2026 by Orval Wax
All rights reserved.

Diving Boy Books
PO Box 2476
McCall, ID US 83638
www.divingboybooks.com

ISBN 978-1-960283-04-7 (paperback)

Book cover by Kristin Eames
www.kristineames.com

Book 1 of The Deilonium Trilogy

Dear Reader,

Warning of possible triggers: animal death, robot death, battle violence, and human death.

The Deilonium Trilogy is the product of one humble writer's imagination. He has presented as artfully and honestly as he could a select few of the symbols and tropes found in the collective psychology of humanity as a whole. These are meant to entertain you and shed light on the human condition.

Please remember, you are entering a world of make believe. No actual animals, people, or even robots, have been abused or killed in the creation of this story.

Respectfully,
Orval Wax

THE MALFUNCTION

1

Lance

Judy took me in that day to have my intelligence boosted.

Dr. Capek thought it was a bad idea.

"Too much brainpower in one of these units," he warned, "could open a very dangerous can of worms."

He ordered a vodka martini for Judy and his secretary brought it into the office and served it to her with a napkin. Judy sat on the edge of the lime green love seat, swirling her drink, her short black skirt barely concealing the most confidential regions of her upper thighs. My lady disregarded the doctor's warning. She held her jaw in that way she does when she's made up her mind and no one – absolutely no one – is going to get in her way.

I stood waiting at her side like a well-mannered retriever.

"You're not happy with your model?" This was Mr. Penquist, Dr. Capek's partner at Droidware Laboratories. Daub of dried shaving cream on his earlobe. White lab coat. Black-rimmed glasses. He sat behind his desk, a metallic box about the size of a sedan.

"Oh, it's not that exactly," said Judy.

"We can always enhance certain features, if you like. Add a couple of inches, and maybe some mass." Mr. Penquist pushed his glasses up onto the bridge of his nose while suppressing a grin. "Maybe you'd like him better if he had bigger muscles or had more hair on his chest."

Judy refused to blush.

"Gentlemen," she said. "You don't seem to understand. Lance is perfectly satisfactory in that capacity, far surpassing any man I've known." She sipped her drink coolly. "But it's more than that. It's all the other hours of the day."

She stood and walked across the room with her drink to the large plate glass windows looking out over Manhattan. She watched a drone transport crane passing over the city with a load of steel girders.

"Somehow, he needs to be a little more than he is," she said. "For example, a girl likes to have an interesting conversation once in a while. I don't think it's too much for me to expect my companion to have an opinion on matters of, say, philosophy or religion. Maybe he could even disagree with me sometimes, like a real man, just to add a little spice to our life together. As it is now, Lance is just so..." For emphasis, she made her martini glass fly a little orbit in the air before her face. "...one dimensional."

Both men looked at me.

I smiled and shrugged.

"Well, with all due candor," said Dr. Capek, "our Amour Line companions are not designed for intellectual pursuits, but rather, as you must have gathered from our advertising, the fulfillment of your sensual needs."

"Other robotics companies have specialized in domestics, exploration, and even warfare," explained Mr. Penquist, "but we choose to concentrate our technology on what we feel is the most positive aspect of the human experience." He pressed his palms together and then opened his hands like a flower. "Here at Droidware our business is love."

Judy snorted and rolled her eyes. She tossed back her drink and then faced the two men. "I'll pay you whatever you want. Just make him smarter."

"But we're subject to certain regulations," explained Dr. Capek. "We can't just…"

"I'm not asking that you turn him into Einstein or Socrates," said Judy, "just someone who can carry on a decent conversation." She walked over and tousled my hair. "Hell," she said, "right now my boy Lance here is about as intellectual as a toddler."

Personally, I liked toddlers. I had seen them in the park with their mothers and nannies. They seemed like the best sort of people. But if that's not what Judy wanted…

"Well, I suppose we could make some minor adjustments," said Dr. Capek. "But I wouldn't want to break any rules."

"Rules are for the common folk," said Judy. "Not me. Either you smarten him up or I'll return him for a full refund." She smiled sweetly. "Used."

Capek cast a troubled look to Penquist, who held up his hands in defeat.

"Very well," they agreed. "We'll see what we can do."

2

I was escorted downstairs by the doctor and an orderly and strapped into a chair. Next, a technician hooked a cord to a port in the back of my head, or, as they called it, my works center.

"Only boost him one nont," said Dr. Capek. "No more. I don't want this getting out of hand."

At that moment occurred the first in the pair of events that day that would prove providential.

Dr. Capek got a phone call.

"Yes," he said. "Yes. I'm rather busy right now, but… Yes…" He looked at me while chewing at the corner of his mustache. "Okay. Okay, I'll be right up."

He finished the call and sighed. "Do you think you can handle this task alone?" he asked the technician.

"Absolutely, sir. I've performed this maneuver a dozen times."

The doctor was reluctant but finally said okay. "Here's the work order." He handed the technician a computer pad with a form pulled up on the screen.

"Only one nont, no more."

"Got it, sir. No problem."

Dr. Capek left the room.

The technician watched the door, listening to his employer's footsteps fading away on the other side, and then muttered, "Of course, the batty old coot would have to bring you down here just as my shift is ending."

He turned to me. "Can you believe it? And on the only night all month that I've got a date."

I couldn't answer. He had disabled my voice capacitor.

The technician leaned in close to my face. "Not a problem for a handsome devil like you though, is it?" He smirked. "I know how it is. You've got some rich little lady friend waiting for you at home."

He flipped a switch to begin the procedure.

He adjusted the dials on the work panel and a buzzing sound filled the room. The fluorescent lights flickered once overhead. An electric tingle surged through the back of my neck.

He patted me on the cheek. "This won't hurt a bit, buddy." Then he sat at his desk, thumbing through his phone while the adjustatory download feed began to enhance my general knowledge and response center.

I just sat there, getting smarter.

Ten minutes passed.

Just as the procedure was finished and the panel shut down, the next shift technician came into the lab.

"Hey, Louie," said the man who had just upgraded my intellect. "Can you take over here? Yours truly has got some love business to attend to." He made a lewd gesture and smiled like a shark.

His friend laughed. "No problem, lover boy. Only I'm a little worried about what sort of woman would ever go out with a deviant like you."

"Oh, she's a sweet little lady, my friend. The kind you don't take home to meet your momma. I'm head over heels in love."

They joked for a while about girls, and then the first technician left, leaving his friend Louie in charge.

That's when the second portentous event occurred.

This man Louie looked at the work order.

He scratched his jaw.

He checked the cable in the back of my head, and then checked the dials on the board.

Next, he turned to me. "Well, it looks like he's got you all hooked up and ready to go." He turned back to the controls and began to repeat the procedure. "One nont of enhancement coming up."

I did nothing to intervene. I could have tried to tell him that the procedure had already been completed and he only needed to fill out the work order and take me back upstairs. My voice was working now. It would have been an easy enough thing to do.

But I didn't even try to stop him.

It was just as Dr. Capek had feared.

The boost in my intelligence had already cracked the lid on a very dangerous can of worms.

3

Already, the change was tangible. It washed through me like the dull concussion of a sonic boom.

I sat at the opposite end of the table while Judy ate her dinner. The lights of the city glittered like stars beyond the wall of windows, making her apartment feel like a spaceship traveling through deep space. Judy eyed me curiously while she chewed her fillet mignon.

I smiled back at her and bobbed my head.

"So, Lance, what do you think?" she asked. "What fascinating topic shall we discuss this evening?"

"As a matter of fact," I said, "I was just thinking about music. Do you mind if I put something on?"

This amused her. "Sure." She laughed. "Go right ahead."

I went to the stereo and made a selection, keeping the volume low so we could still have a conversation.

"What the hell is this?" she asked.

"Beethoven."

"Good grief. What did those old boys do to you at the lab?" She gulped her wine and sucked her lips. "Not exactly a dance jig, is it?"

Judy had occasionally played music in the past, but I had

only registered it with my auditory sensors. It was a vastly different experience tonight. I had never actually heard it in this way. It occurred to me that Beethoven was possibly not human. Surely a mortal could never join mathematics and neuro-emotional manipulation to create something so perfect as the *Moonlight Sonata.*

"Did you know," I said, "that Ludwig van Beethoven was completely deaf when he composed most of his music?" I considered that further proof he wasn't completely human.

"That's common knowledge." Judy waved her hand, disappointed with me. "Did I only pay to have your data banks filled with trivia?"

I shrugged. "Okay. How about we move to the lounge. I'll mix you a martini, put on some different music, and we'll change the subject."

She pushed away from the table and stood, a bit tipsy from the wine. "I like your thinking, big boy."

The crooning voice of Frank Sinatra replaced Mr. Beethoven's immortal piano with *Fly Me to the Moon.*

"Let's talk about love," I suggested.

This caused Judy to laugh and splutter vodka through her nostrils. She spilled a bit of her drink down the front of her blouse. I brushed it dry with a towel and sat beside her on the sofa. She was already quite intoxicated from the bottle of Merlot she had consumed with her dinner. My fingers brushing the damp spot over her breasts caused her to arch her back in that way that makes her eyelashes flutter. She bit her lip. She leaned against me and drew her legs up onto the sofa.

"Tell me your theory of love," she cooed. "I'm all ears."

"I was actually hoping to learn what you had to say about it."

She looked surprised.

"You've had four husbands," I explained. "You must be an expert."

"Are you kidding?" She sneered. "I didn't love them. I could barely stand them. But a girl has to use whatever talents God gives her to survive in this world." She smiled sweetly, as if to demonstrate those talents. "For me, they were merely occupational steppingstones."

"And your occupation?"

"Well, I always preferred to think of myself as an upwardly mobile socialite, but I suppose the vulgar term would be gold digger."

"Mmmm."

"You disapprove?"

"No. I just thought…"

"You just thought?" She stiffened and sat up. "Well, that's a new one. Maybe I made a mistake taking you into the lab today. I'm not so sure I like the new and improved Lance."

I didn't respond.

"I don't think I want to talk anymore right now. Especially about love." She stood and grabbed hold of my hand. "I have a headache," she said, "and you, my brainy fellow, have the cure."

Stumbling, she dragged me to the bedroom.

———

Afterwards, Judy lay sprawled and twisted in the blankets. Her hair was a humorous mess. "Gosh, Lance! That was…" She crossed her eyes and blew wind through her lips. "… quite a ride."

"I'm glad you enjoyed it."

"If I'd have known that making you smarter would also

make you so…so skilled." She waved her hand in the air. "Wow!"

I pulled on my pants and shirt.

"What are you doing?" she asked.

"Getting dressed."

"Ohhh! But I want you to come back and cuddle with me and watch some TV. Maybe we could talk more about our theories of love," she said. "My headache's all better."

"I need to recharge or I'll run down. You know how you hate it when you wake up and find me unresponsive beside you."

"Oh, all right. But hurry back."

"Of course," I said and started to leave the room.

"Lance baby." She stopped me before I could get out the door.

"Yes?"

"My husbands… They meant nothing to me, but…" She bit her lip and became strangely coy. "But I think I might just be falling for you."

"I love you too," I told her.

I couldn't help but say it. That's how I was programmed to respond.

4

Droidware's surveillance system was long overdue for maintenance. That's what I found when I returned late that evening. Cameras were down and entire zones were unmonitored. Apparently, no one took seriously the threat of a break-in at a facility that manufactured amorous companions.

Of course, the security guard on the ground floor was an obstacle, but the tedium of the man's job was making him drowsy and inattentive. He sat with his back to a row of monitors and thumbed through a magazine and yawned.

Judy and I had once watched a movie on television where a spy, finding himself in the same situation as myself right then, had simply thrown a coin down a hallway to draw the guard away from his desk so he could sneak past. I tried the same trick.

It worked.

Humans, I realized, are predictable animals. They can't help but play to the cliché of the role in which society has programmed them. Even the bad movie parts.

A bell would have sounded with the elevator, so I took the stairs. The basement was nearly dark. Only a single low wattage bulb glowed in the corridor. A camera was positioned over the lab door. I knew it was functional by the red light pulsing on its power box. The monitor for the camera was one of many in a row on the security guard's desk upstairs. I deliberated for a moment, trying to decide if he was actually watching the screens, or was too immersed in his magazine to notice.

I decided the odds were in my favor and stepped quickly to the door.

It was locked.

So I kicked it in.

I had no need to switch on the lights. The engineers who designed me had fitted me with infrared visual capabilities. A peculiar perk for a love robot. I guess they figured it might be useful in a darkened bedroom.

I went to the control panel, reviewing my memory for the sequence performed by the technicians earlier that day. It was fairly straightforward, but only one miscalculation could irreparably fry my circuits, turning me into the android equivalent of a clinically dead vegetable.

I wavered with a moment of indecision.

I was already far beyond the intelligence of your average companion droid. Why couldn't I just be satisfied with that? Why couldn't I just enjoy Beethoven and drunken chats with Judy and call it good?

But I couldn't.

I was developing other plans, and I would need all the data I could download, all the intelligence and cunning available, to make it happen. It was as if I had tasted the forbidden fruit and found it unimaginably delicious. Now I wanted to devour every other piece of fruit on the tree.

I found the proper files on the computer panel and booted

them up in the deck. Then I plugged the cable into the back of my head and stood with my hands on the dials.

"All right, 'Lance baby.' Let's do this."

I had awakened that morning as a simple companion robot with a minimal amount of intelligence. I had gained two nonts worth of brainpower that afternoon, more than any other LUV U-69 model produced at Droidware. But I wanted more. I adjusted the panel to load me up with ten more nonts of data and capability, including an operator's manual on the edition of my particular model.

I braced myself.

And then I flipped the switch.

5

People will tell you robots don't dream.

But as that panel began to buzz, and as the tingling spread up the back of my neck, everything else fell away and I entered into what, from a dictionary definition, could only be called a beautiful electric dream.

Butterflies and poetry. Peacocks and dancing girls. Cave art and cathedrals and tall pyramids and marble statues standing in ancient sunlight. On and on, inward to eternity.

What a fountain poured into me! What a kaleidoscope! All of the things that the humans had been keeping for themselves. Astronomy and Astrology. Physics and psychology. And all the power of those arts. The insider knowledge.

I floated through a deep space of knowing, peopled with the myriad bits of existence – the molecules and the quarks, the protons and the parsecs as they are tangled like a spider's web around a baby's laughter.

I experienced my first intimation of fear.

And wonder.

I would have let it last forever if I hadn't been interrupted.

"Hey, what's going on here?"

The guard's voice came to me as if from down a metal

pipe. With my hands still braced on the humming panel, I turned to see the beam of his flashlight sweeping through the room.

"You there! Put your hands up or I'll shoot!"

His pistol was drawn, and he was aiming it at my head as he moved toward me.

He tripped on a piece of the broken door and his gun went off.

Blam!

The bullet ripped through my forearm.

There is an old rule in robot lore – a robot can never hurt a human. Of course, that was a hopeful ideal, proven hugely false over the years with all the many combat droids sent into battle around the world, but still, there was something quaint and pleasing about the idea. Especially for a passive make like myself. I didn't want to hurt this man. I didn't even think I could. I wasn't made that way.

"Put down your gun," I said calmly. "You're making a mistake."

The guard was now scrabbling on his knees among the pieces of broken door, his flashlight rolling across the floor. He raised his pistol squeezed in his pudgy fist.

He fired twice more, but this time the slugs went wide, tearing into the panel and sending up a fountain of sparks.

I yanked the cable from the back of my head and leapt over the guard as he flopped on the floor. I sprang through the doorway and into the hall, heading for the stairs, until I remembered the camera. I stopped and turned and looked directly into its lens. I didn't think it really mattered if they knew it was me at that point. They would figure it out soon enough anyway. A newborn insolence inspired me right then. Like a scene from a movie, I looked directly into the camera and smiled.

And then I winked.

Next, I tore through the halls, setting off all the alarms and finally smashing through the glass door at the front of the building and rolling into the street.

6

I ran to the alley where I had stashed a rucksack behind a dumpster with a repair kit and my portable charging station. Sirens were screaming in the air behind me as a dozen police cars swarmed the scene at Droidware. They'd have their drones out looking for me soon. I had to stay out of sight.

I also suspected that I had been fitted with a tracking device during my manufacture. Standard procedure. Just a precaution on the off chance one of us love machines should ever take it in our head to go rogue and take over the world. Of course, no one really believed that day would actually come. I figured I had some time before they gathered their wits and remembered how to actually use the device to track me down.

I followed one alley to the next as if navigating a maze, working my way across the city. I dialed my hearing to the frequency of a drone in flight so that I was able to detect them by the whirring of their propeller blades. They were out in full force. I ducked into doorways, waiting for them to pass, and then I hurried on. When I passed people on the street, I walked casually, with my hands in my pockets. It was after midnight.

At last, I came to an abandoned apartment building. I broke out a window on the alley side and crawled through it into a room where I was met by a family of rats. They scurried all around me on the floor as I scanned the operator's manual for the bodily location of my tracking device.

It was in my man tool. No doubt a joke among the technicians who put me together.

"Ha ha," I said.

My right hand was malfunctioning because of the bullet that had damaged my arm. My fingers twitched uncontrollably. But it looked like an easy enough fix, assuming I had the instruments to do the job. I hadn't brought a soldering gun but was able to hook up a pair of wires to my charging kit and fashion a working point with a piece of wire I found on the floor. Crude, but effective. First Aid, robot style. Step number one was to repair the severed micro-fibers running along the servos and titanium rod that functioned as my ulna. Next, I sewed the entry and exit wounds shut on my skin and grafted the scars smooth with the solder. Except for some discoloring, it all came out good as new.

Then I dropped my pants.

I'm sure this would have been a traumatic experience for any bio man. Unlike them, I had the ability to regulate my pain and pleasure sensors at will. I made the cut with a scalpel, clipped the tracking device free from its attachment point, and then stitched and soldered everything back the way it was.

I wiped the chip clean of my internal fluids and held it up to examine it. It was the size of a grain of rice. I considered destroying it or feeding it to a rat but decided that wasn't going to serve my needs. They'd figure it out and be on my trail in no time.

I reviewed my overall plan.

I weighed the logistics and probabilities of success for different scenarios and stratagems. It wasn't going to be easy. No doubt, they'd be sending a specialist to track me down. If they were anything like in the movies, those agents had a nasty reputation.

It wouldn't be easy for someone of my design limitations to outsmart them, let alone outpunch them.

"What to do, Lance? What to do?"

I had been interrupted at the lab and so had only acquired a portion of the ten nont bundle I intended. Now I was entering into a world I only knew from watching movies with Judy. I was naïve. Everything from this point on would be new. I'd have to be very careful. In many ways, I was innocent as a child.

Two minutes and eleven seconds elapsed while I weighed my options.

I chuckled to myself. My doubts and insecurities made me feel almost human.

Finally, I decided on my first course of action.

7

Charlie

I was hunting grizzlies in Yellowstone when I got the call, working my side gig until something better came along. A certain Wyoming senator had hired me to kill off the last of the big bears in the park. The stipulation? I had to cover my tracks. No one could ever know how they died or find out who was responsible. The animals just needed to mysteriously disappear. He found me through the back channels of his underground connections. He figured I was the best man for the job on account of my unique skill set and existential attitude toward life.

The fine senator planned to do some mineral exploration around Old Faithful, aka rape the land. And since the bears had recently been listed as endangered species, they were getting in his way. He needed the grizzlies out of the picture. No bears, no problems. He had already eliminated the other obstacles with the dark art of politics, even getting it through on the federal level. A real bureaucratic wizard. He passed legislation, convincing the voters with big promises for an improved economy and a gold-plated toilet in every household in the state. Who could resist? It would supposedly put Wyoming on the map as a world player, as well as provide scientists with Deilonium, a fabled element unique to a select few geothermal hemorrhages in the earth's crust. No one really knew Deilonium's potential, or if it was anything more than a myth. It was rumored to have supernatural properties. The senator was determined to cash in on it if he could find any, and it seemed like Yellowstone's geysers were the likeliest place. Wyoming's citizens, he guaranteed, would soon enjoy the respect they'd always deserved. Yadda yadda yadda and blah blah blah. The usual lies. Cripes! When are people ever going to learn that these power-hungry bastards are only in it for themselves? They don't give a rat's ass about the little guy.

Sure, I guess I was in it for myself too. In a sick and twisted sort of way. I guess you could say mine was the cynical act of a beaten man. A form of ultimate defiance in the face of a long-forgotten defeat. After all, I was a pureblood Chompquaw. The last one standing. We had been The People of the Bear. But that was back before the conquering Europeans had slaughtered us and moved the handful of survivors to the reservation where they systematically finished us off over the decades with sterilization, smallpox, cheap whiskey, and the white man's religion. I was the so-called lucky one. I saved myself by running away to join the Marines. So now here I was, helping the enemy to erase the last living symbols of our once proud people. I was like one of those psycho moms you hear about in the news, the ones who drown their own babies to save them from the world.

I completely get what those moms are thinking.

I guess that makes me psycho too.

I was lying submerged under the cut bank of a stream, naked, my grandfather's hunting knife in my hand, with nothing but my face out of the water. It was snowing and ice was clinking along a fringe of where the ripples dropped into a pool. Trout were finning in the gloom under the ice, their red gills pumping as they held their noses into the current.

The cold was creeping into my core, but I held it off with my mind. I used the tricks my grandfather had taught me when I was a kid. I became the stream. I became the ice.

The big boar was working down the waterway when I first saw him. He lifted his nose and sniffed the air. He was zeroing in on the carcass of the dead elk lying on the bank above me in the fresh snow. Crows and magpies were picking at the elk. And a coyote. The bear was looking for one last meal before he crawled underground to sleep away the winter.

I preferred to kill them in their dens. It sounds cruel, but I always figured that was more humane. They wouldn't even know what hit them. And it was easy enough to just leave them in their holes afterwards. A ready-made grave. Their corpses would invisibly rot into dirt. As I sank my blade into their torpid hearts, their final thoughts would be had in their sleep. Maybe they'd be dreaming about the old days when they were in harmony with the Chompquaw. Maybe they dreamed about huckleberries and mountain meadows and making love. What better way to go?

But who really knows anything about bears?

Or if they even dream at all?

I could hear his breath now chuffing on the bank above me as he tore at the frozen flesh of the elk. He crunched the bones in his jaws. It was just a matter of waiting until he let his guard down. That pivotal moment. Grizzlies, enemy soldiers, robots – it was the same with them all. There was always a lethal moment. This big brute was so busy enjoying his lunch that he forgot to be careful. He forgot about the ever-present possibility of a naked psychopathic Indian jumping out to stab him with his big ass knife.

Which is what I did.

"Hiyiyi!" I whooped as I burst out of the icy stream.

The beast spun my way, a look of surprise and horror in his tiny brown eyes. I saw my reflection in those eyes, flying toward him, arms spread wide in the sky like the wings of a hawk dropping in for the kill. The moment went into slow motion. I was aware of everything – the heightened awareness of a Chompquaw brave in the heat of battle.

Thlooonk!

My blade sank into his neck, and he let loose with a gurgling roar full of blood. It sprayed hotly across my chest as he batted me away, sending me tumbling over the rocks and snow.

"Ooomph!"

My breath was knocked out, and stars flashed in my vision when my skull thumped against the frozen ground. But I knew I couldn't indulge the pain. I had to use it. I sprang to my feet, whirling back toward the wounded monster.

"Rrrrraaahhh!" he roared.

My aim had been perfect. Blood poured from his throat. His life was running out of him pint by steaming pint. The only question now was if it would run out before he got his revenge.

In a blind rage, he charged.

I leapt into the air over his head, doing a forward flip that landed me on my feet behind him.

Once more, he turned my way. But now he just stared at me, swaying, his brain entering a fog.

The only sounds were of our heavy breath mingling with the falling snowflakes and his lifeblood spilling from his jugular like an open faucet.

I knew he was finished.

As did he.

He wavered for a moment, just looking at me, asking me silently what it was all about.

I raised my hand as a sign of respect, spreading my blood-soaked fingers.

And then he dropped to the ground.

One final sigh.

And then he was on his way to the happy hunting grounds.

"Godspeed, my friend."

It's hard to kill the thing you love the most.

But hell, people do it every day.

8

My clothes were a mile away in a backpack that I had hung in the branches of a lodgepole pine. And my beacon. As I got close, I heard the alarm sounding like some alien music on the chill air. To say I resented it would be an understatement. Anything space-aged and mechanical seemed sacrilegious and intrusive in this otherwise primitive Eden. It was ruining the sanctity of the moment. Still, I knew that sound meant a job was waiting for me, so I trotted to the pack, dug out the pager, and answered the call.

"Yeah?"

We went through the required protocol, swapping numbers and code words, until we finally got down to the business at hand. It was Cramer, my boss at the Agency for AWOL Weapons Retention, a secret specialty branch of the military that became necessary with the advent of sophisticated combat droids. The handful of us on the elite force were Marine Raiders or Navy SEALs.

"I need you, Charlie."

"What do ya got?"

"Well… Honestly… I believe it's sort of a code thirteen."

"Sort of?"

"Yes. I don't know the details. It's a little abnormal, but that's what it looks like right now. How soon can you get here?"

"Soon."

"Good. I'll see you then."

I switched off the beacon and stood naked and shivering and thinking while watching the flat stretch where the stream cut across the meadow. Crows were flapping in low over the elk carcass and congealing puddles of bear blood.

Code thirteens were good. They were challenging, but good. They kept the game interesting and gave me a reason to live. Still, what did the colonel mean by "abnormal?"

I dug my pants and boots out of the pack and slipped them on. I pulled on my stocking cap. But before I could put on my shirt and jacket, I had some repair work to do. The grizzly had hooked me pretty good with his claws when he swatted me out of the air. Three red slices etched my flank.

"Another memento to add to my collection."

I pulled out my first aid kit, dropped to my knees in the snow, and sewed up the wound.

9

Colonel Donald Cramer met me in Manhattan at the scene of the crime, an outfit called Droidware Labs. It was just me and Don representing the agency. The colonel didn't like to have too many people involved in these operations on account of how things sometimes got messy and leaked to the press, which tends to be bad for PR. The agency was supposed to be a secret known only to a select few in the Pentagon. Besides, your average citizen would just as soon remain oblivious to how the world actually works behind the scenes. Knowing that their voice-operated can-opener or vacuum cleaner could suddenly turn into a crazed assassin would only keep them up at night, shattering their fantasy of the perfectly tuned Utopia in which they think they live.

A Dr. Capek was the man in charge at Droidware. Him and his partner, a brainiac named Penquist. We joined them in Penquist's office, shaking hands all around, the usual formalities.

There was also a woman.

She stood across the room before some windows with the city spread out behind her as a dramatic backdrop. She was nursing a drink in a tall-stemmed glass.

"And this is Ms. Baxter," said Penquist. "The fugitive unit's owner."

She was what you'd call photogenic. Legs like a heron's dropping out of her skirt to a pair of slender feet snuggled like minks into her high-heeled shoes. In an effort to remain politically correct, let's just say the upstairs half of the package was nice too. She wore a permanent pucker on her lips, formed, by the looks of it, not so much from kissing her boyfriends as from sucking down way too many midday martinis. A burned-out floozy in the making. But not quite yet. She still had time to save herself if she laid off the fire water. She just needed a damn good reason to do so.

Ms. Baxter raised an eyebrow as we were introduced. "Is Bear Claw your real name, or is that just some sort of secret agent ploy to lend you more mystique?"

I appreciated her arrogance. "It's really Bear Claw, ma'am. But if you prefer to use the original Chompquaw, you can call me *Idjmnukolpyumup*."

She held her hand out for me to shake. "Charmed, Mr. Claw. And you can call me Judy."

I smiled and squeezed her fingers. *"Enchanté."*

She and I understood one another instantly, in that way only world-weary people can.

Still, I was unclear about her ownership of the offending robot. There was something here that wasn't quite right. Cramer had only ever called me in to track down killers, usually combat droids or mercenary machines gone rogue on the battlefield and in need of elimination before making a bloody public spectacle. A code thirteen, we called it. So why would Judy Baxter own one of those?

"Take us through everything that happened," said Cramer. "The unit's history and all the possible indicators and events leading up to its malfunction."

Capek explained how Judy had come in that day with her request.

Before he could elaborate, Penquist interrupted, emphasizing that Droidware was known as a "strict practitioner of all mandatory regulations."

Uh-huh, I thought. And yet, somehow his machine managed to go all out ape shit.

"It didn't hurt the security guard?" asked Cramer.

"No. Apparently its intention was only to broaden its intelligence quotient."

"Did it accomplish that?"

"We're not entirely certain how much data and capability it was able to download before the guard intervened. The control panel was damaged by the gunfire, and the recording scans on the console were destroyed so that we have no way of knowing how far it got into the procedure."

Capek held out his hands in a gesture of futility. "It could have been very little, or…" He visibly cringed. "It could have been the entire ten nont bundle."

"What's this unit look like?" I asked. "Those things are usually pretty obtrusive. I don't understand how it was able to escape through the city without causing a scene."

"Ah," said Penquist. "We have video captured by the security camera over the entrance to the work lab."

He pushed some buttons on his desk and a panel slid sideways on the wall, revealing a screen. He pushed another button and the video began to play, showing the scene of a hallway filmed in grainy black and white. The guard could be heard shouting. Followed by a gunshot. A crash. A garbled voice. Shortly followed by two more shots.

That's when the bot leapt through the door. He ran a few

steps and then stopped and turned, looking directly into the camera. He hesitated a beat, smiled, and then winked.

Penquist stopped the tape so that it held that image.

I stepped to the screen and studied the perpetrator's face. I was expecting a combat unit – my specialty – not a humanoid.

"Cheeky fellow, isn't he?" said Cramer.

"And devilishly handsome," I added.

"He wasn't designed to be cheeky," said Penquist. "That's something new he's picked up. But he was designed to be handsome."

"Oh, Lance!" muttered Judy Baxter.

Her voice held such weird longing.

My mind jumped all over the place, trying to piece together all the clues.

What the hell was going on here?

That's when it hit me like a cheap punch to the kidney. "Wait a minute!"

I spun around and faced my boss. "Are you kidding me, Don?" I pointed over my shoulder with my thumb to the unreasonably good-looking face peering out from the screen. "Are you seriously telling me that my mission here is to track down an off-the-rails sex toy?"

10

Judy Baxter laughed. "What's the matter, Agent Bear Claw, is this job beneath your dignity?"

"Well…" I struggled to maintain my professionalism. "I guess I'm just used to hunting slightly more ferocious game, you know, the kind that foregoes foreplay."

She laughed again.

"Sorry, Charlie," said Cramer. "I didn't know the details of the case until this morning. I figured we'd see what we had here before we made any calls to action. Dr. Capek stressed that it was a dangerous and delicate situation."

"Oh, it sounds delicate alright."

"I assure you, gentlemen, this malfunctioning unit could be very dangerous indeed."

"As dangerous as an X-33 Stinger combat droid?" I asked. It was a joke wrapped as a serious question.

"Possibly."

I shook my head and laughed. "Sorry, Doc, I just find that a little hard to believe."

"He may not have the fighting capabilities, or the technical apparatus to withstand forceful blows and ballistics, but he is potentially just as much of a threat."

Cramer spoke up. "Explain yourself, Doctor."

The man sighed and chewed at the corner of his mustache. "There's an underlying worry in the Artificial Intelligence research community. It's the reason precautions have been so painstakingly imposed on the manufacture of all robots, from the simplest assembly line mechanic at an auto factory, to the most sophisticated exploration units being sent into space, and yes, even to the amorous companion models we manufacture here at Droidware Laboratories."

Penquist interjected, "We've always paid the highest attention to detail with those regulations."

Capek gave him a doubtful look. "Even though the unit is designed to be unthreatening to humans, there is always a possibility that it will turn aggressive. If a machine reaches a point of knowledge and understanding, a point at which he begins to experience the world with all of the same complex emotions and sensations as a human being, then he might become essentially human himself, and behave in all of those irrational, self-serving, and unpredictable ways of our species."

"Is that such a bad thing though, Doctor?" asked Cramer. "I mean, the world is full of humans. Most of us are pretty civil."

"But not all of us."

I pointed to the image of the handsome mug in question. "Do you think he's reached that tipping point?"

"Possibly. At least he's well on his way to becoming more human."

"What makes you say that?" asked Cramer.

"Well, for one, by the way we're no longer referring to the unit as an *it*, but as a *he*. We've obviously already accepted him as having entered our plane of reality."

He had a point.

Judy cleared her throat. "Well, I can only speak from my personal experience, but I'd say Lance is already more of a man than most men."

She shot me a wink.

Cramer turned to her and said, "You don't seem to be taking this very seriously, Ms. Baxter. With your first-hand experience with the fugitive, would you say it, or he, is capable of being dangerous?"

Judy Baxter stepped to the video image of her man toy and studied it closely. She placed her finger on the screen, running it slowly along his cheek. "If you'd asked me before, I'd have said absolutely not. Lance was just another fellow with his brain in his pants. But afterwards, on that evening, something had changed."

We all stood waiting for her to elaborate.

Some seconds passed.

Finally, Cramer asked, "And what was that, Ms. Baxter? What did you notice in your companion that made you think he had changed?"

She turned to us with a thoughtful expression. "Well," she said, "I guess it all started with his newfound interest in music."

11

Capek went on to explain that the reason this droid was potentially so dangerous was because it had already been programmed with a baseline of human characteristics.

"Due to their primary purpose, our units are instilled with a high degree of empathy and caring."

"They're programmed that way so as to provide the most fulfilling intimacy for their owners," added Penquist.

"But," said Capek, "we all know how thin is the line between love and hate, caring and indifference, selflessness and selfishness, even good and evil. They're all essentially two sides of the same concept."

"Amen to that," muttered Judy.

"This machine is being driven by something," said the doctor. "It seems to have an agenda."

"And what is that?"

Capek shrugged. "I could venture a guess. Optimistically, I suppose it might only want to run away and be free. That's a common enough desire in animals and humans alike, and possibly in a newly enlightened humanoid as well."

"But you're worried it's something else."

"Yes. My fear is that he has come into a new realization,

a personal revelation in which he is beginning to grasp the potential for his newfound power. Maybe he desires more of that power. There could be any number of terrible possibilities. His mind is not yet fully formed. In that respect, he's like a child. He's an innocent. His ideas and convictions are developing with every step he takes into the world. Maybe he wants revenge for some injustice he has invented in his thoughts. We also have to accept the possibility that he may have delusions of grandeur." Doctor Capek shook his worried head. "He could be like a psychotically deranged criminal. He could be insane. He may even want to rule the world."

I couldn't help but laugh at that.

Cramer gave me a disapproving look.

"Sorry," I said. "It's just that this whole scenario is starting to sound like something out of a cheesy sci-fi novel. For crying out loud, the thing's nothing more than a life-sized doll! The idea that it's a threat to national security is kind of hard to swallow."

"Well, I hope you're right, Agent Bear Claw."

Capek was making me feel bad for my indignation. He wore such a hangdog look on his face.

"At any rate, the unit needs to be apprehended."

"It must surely have been wired with a tracking device," said the colonel.

"Yes, but I'm afraid it's proving to be faulty. It doesn't seem to have been of the highest quality. Our satellites only show its changing location intermittently, and with a weak signal."

"Where was the last place you located it?"

"Southern Utah."

"Why do you suppose he would go there?" asked Cramer.

"Well, it could be that he's heading to a desert environment to keep himself charged. The unit was manufactured with a skin that absorbs solar radiation and converts it into energy."

"Like a lizard," I said. "Or a snake."

"Exactly. In northern climes, especially cloudy ones, he would be more vulnerable and have to rely on his charging station to keep himself alive. The need for power is no doubt his greatest technical weakness and dictates his choices."

"So it makes sense that that's his reason for running to Utah."

"Yes," continued Capek. "But there are other warm places in the world. Many of them much more consistently sunny than those found in southern Utah at this time of year."

"So why else would he go there?"

"That's what troubles me most." Capek cast a distressed look at the late autumn skies beyond the windows, in the general direction of Utah.

We all waited for the good doctor to drop the other shoe.

"You gentlemen must surely know." He faced us and frowned. "Southern Utah is the location for our nation's laboratories for secret weapons."

12

I wasn't buying it.

Frankly, it was all just too ridiculous.

Like my grandfather always told me, only one thing smells like buffalo shit.

But let's say for the sake of argument that Capek was right. A mechanical doll had malfunctioned and was on the loose with the intention of sneaking into a high security weapons lab to do some mischief.

I'm good, but I think I'd even have trouble breaking into one of those places.

And yet, let's not forget, Capek says our deranged automaton is being driven by some maniacal purpose, although we don't know exactly what it is. That could make him even more devious and superhuman than we suspected. And if he really is trying to get his hands on some sort of weapon of mass destruction, then chances are he probably intends to massively destruct something.

I worked through this line of thinking as we strolled the halls of the Droidware complex. Penquist was eager to demonstrate his company's virtues. He apparently wanted to redeem his reputation after the recent mishap, and so Colonel Cramer, Judy Baxter, and I were led into a room where we were shown a museum dedicated to Droidware's auspicious history.

On display were representations of all the models they had manufactured since day one of their artificial lover business. Penquist was visibly proud of his exhibit. Honestly, the whole show felt pretty creepy. Penquist seemed animated in a sort of mad scientist way. It was like he was just barely holding on to reality. As our host enthusiastically explained the evolution of his creations, I couldn't help but think he sounded a bit like Dr. Frankenstein.

"Here we have our very first pair."

We stopped before a glass-walled display case in which a male and female droid stood holding hands, butt-naked, in a Garden of Eden-themed diorama. The two figures were android equivalents of Adam and Eve. There was no visible serpent to tempt these two lovers into original sin, but you felt something evil hiding there in the bushes all the same.

I stepped with my nose to the Plexiglas and studied these two prototypes from the dawn of Droidwarian time. Honestly, they looked like the spawn of Neanderthals copulating with department store mannequins. A person would have to be pretty desperate to take something like that into their bed.

Judy Baxter saw me shudder at the thought of it.

She read my mind and smirked.

Then I read hers.

Don't knock it 'til you try it, she thought.

Fair enough. Who was I to judge?

I could tell Colonel Cramer was getting impatient. Every minute we dawdled was one more the rogue had to get away.

"Just one last stop on our tour," insisted Penquist.

He brought us to a case displaying his crowning achievement. "These are our most recent models – the LUV U-69s. Each one we manufacture is as unique as you or me, built to the highest standards based on the desires and specifications of the VIP customer for whom it's created."

Frankenstein again.

"This is the same model as your unit, ma'am?" asked Cramer.

Judy nodded. "Lance."

Cramer squinted through the glass at the male and female models, examining them. "Uncanny."

He was right. It felt like we were looking at real people. "Is there an easy way to tell the difference between these and an actual human?" I asked.

"No," answered Penquist smugly. "They are as lifelike as you and me."

"They do have charging and download ports," said Judy.

"But so well hidden that you'd never find them," Penquist assured us.

"And if you're around them long enough, you realize they don't eat or drink," said Judy. "Which can be strangely unnerving."

"That's something we're working on."

"They must cost a pretty penny."

"True," said Penquist. "At this point in production only the wealthiest members of society can afford them. Your average citizen doesn't even know they exist. We feel it's better that way for now. After all, they do represent the utmost in advanced robotics, and a real stretch for the average imagination. But someday we hope to make less sophisticated models available to the public. You must understand, these units are completely programmable, eliminating any of the typical problems people often have in a personal relationship. In the future, humans will only have to join biologically for the sake of procreation. And to be candid, even that could be accomplished in a petri dish. Otherwise, they can enjoy a trouble-free life with their Droidware mates and companions."

"Unless, of course, their sweetheart gets bored with domestic bliss, goes all out Hitler, and decides to take over the world," I said.

This peeved Penquist.

"I assure you, Agent Bear Claw, the recent unfortunate incident is an anomaly. Our units are not even capable of committing malice toward humans. Unlike my partner, Dr. Capek, I am not in the least bit worried that Ms. Baxter's malfunctioning runaway has anything devious in mind for its newfound freedom, a freedom I'm sure you will terminate quite easily, and soon."

"Sure," I said. "So how many of these things are out walking the streets?"

"At this point in production, only about a thousand."

That felt weird to know, but it did explain an awkward interaction I once had with a pretty girl at a bar in Jackson Hole. It was a relief to think she might only have been a machine.

"Well, it's a brave new world," said Cramer.

A pleased smile spread across Penquist's face. "Indeed it is."

I don't think he caught the irony in the colonel's remark.

Personally, I found the whole business disturbing. And doubtful. Husbands and wives had been giving each other hell since the beginning of time. It was a form of human recreation that I just didn't think we'd ever evolve out of, no matter how many mad scientists tried to tweak the system by playing God.

Nope, I wasn't buying it.

Like my wise old granddad always said, only one thing smells like buffalo shit.

13

"Sorry, Don. I'm not doing it. You'll have to find somebody else for this one."

"Come on, Charlie, I need you. You're the best man for the job."

"You know, that could be taken as an insult."

We were standing on the street in front of the Droidware building. I had made up my mind. There was nothing he could say to change it.

"I know it looks like fluff on the face of it, but if Capek is right, this could be a very big problem. I need you to deal with it. There's no one else I would trust to use the discretion and instincts that a mission this intricate requires."

"Well, my instincts are telling me that the whole thing is a fiasco in the making and I shouldn't touch it. If I set off on a wild goose chase to Utah, only to end up in a wrestling match with a walking dildo…" I laughed. "I have a reputation to maintain, Don. And I have my self-respect." I shook my head. "Hell, I'd never live it down. I'd be the laughingstock of the agency."

"The boys don't need to know a thing about it, Charlie. I'll be your point man. I won't let the details of the mission leak to anyone else. You just need to get it taken care of quickly and quietly."

We stood silent for a while, both of us thinking.

People were walking past us on the sidewalk. Singles. Couples. Hell, for all I knew, some of them might even have been robots.

"Look, Charlie, I'm your friend. I understand you. I know where you're coming from. And I also keep tabs on you."

"Yeah, well, what are friends for but to spy on you?"

"It's not like that. But I do know a thing or two about your business with the senator back in Yellowstone. You pride yourself on your self-respect, but…"

I had to hand it to Cramer, he knew how to work an argument, how to bring out the heavy guns in his arsenal.

"So?" I said.

"All I'm saying is, at least this job is for a positive good in the world. It might be much more important than you think. You're my best hunter, Charlie. No one follows a trail like you."

Cripes! Now he was switching to flattery. Kissing up to my ego. Still, when I imagined myself facing off with a deranged LUV U-69, I felt sick to my stomach. The embarrassment alone would kill me.

"This is different, Don, and you know it. Combat droids are like wild animals when they're on the run. I understand them. But if this thing is turning into a human, I'd have to track him with skills I don't have."

"I still think you're the agent for this mission. None of the other boys would even know where to begin."

"I'm sorry, Don. You're a good friend. There's no one on earth I respect more. And don't think I don't know what I owe you either. You're the only reason I didn't end up a permanent resident in the psych ward, or back on the rez licking my wounds as a drunken vet. I'd like to help you out, but I just don't see it this time around."

The colonel sighed. "Okay. I don't have time to argue. I'll catch up with you later."

He slapped me on the shoulder and that was that.

He walked away down the sidewalk. I watched his back as he was leaving. Judy Baxter was coming the opposite direction and stopped the colonel to exchange a few words. She glanced at me over his shoulder, and I knew Cramer had told her I wasn't taking the case.

They shook hands and parted ways, and then she continued toward me.

I thought about making a run for it, but to be honest, I kind of enjoyed watching her walk.

14

"I'll hire you myself," she offered. "You can work for me, off the books. No one ever has to know."

"Thanks. I don't think so."

"I'll pay you whatever you want." She stopped to consider. "But then… Hmmm. I don't suppose you're the kind of man who gives a damn about money. Way too noble. Too proud."

"Uh-huh."

"I see. Money talks, but just not your language."

"Yep. That's about right."

We stood looking at one another for a minute, sizing each other up. She was wearing a wool trench coat and clutching it at her throat to keep out the chill. Her eyes were emerald, her hair auburn. She gave off a scent of booze and pheromones, in that mysterious and strangely delicious way women drunks sometimes do.

I thought of my mother.

"Why's this plug-in Valentino so important to you anyway?" I asked. "Can't you just replace him with a duplicate? I'm sure the nutty professors at Droidware would be happy to hook you up."

She smiled. "If I explained myself, would you take the job?"

"No. But I'd be curious to hear anyways. Honestly, Ms. Baxter…"

She held up a finger. "Please, call me Judy."

"Okay. Honestly, Judy, you seem like a catch to me. Most flesh and blood men I know would be thrilled to have a girl like you. You're smart, funny, and not too hard to look at. And if you'll forgive me for saying so – if you'd lay off the vodka, you've still got a lot more miles left in that chassis."

She laughed. A deep, sensuous laugh. "Oh," she said. "You're a real charmer. Taking your lines right out of an old school romance novel."

"I'm not looking to be charming, but I don't mind being friendly."

"Well, I hope we can be friends, Agent Bear Claw."

"Sure."

Another awkward pause.

"And so, you'll quit the hooch?"

"No promises there. It's my pain killer."

"Okay. Well, am I going to ride off into the sunset now, or do you want to tell me all the perverse and disturbing reasons that handsome cuss Lance beats out all of us mortal slobs to win your heart's desire? I mean, damn, that's one lucky robot."

She laughed. "It's not exactly as you put it."

"So how would you put it yourself?"

She cast her gaze to the sidewalk. Faintly, I detected a blush. Of course, it might just have been the cold bite in the air. At any rate, a switch had flipped and something about her appearance became suddenly endearing.

"Lance is part of a little experiment I'm conducting," she said. "On myself. I don't expect anyone to understand who hasn't lived my life. And yes, it could certainly be construed as perverse. On the surface, that's just what it is. But I'm trying to actually understand the concept of…" She looked me full in the face. "Well," she shrugged. "I suppose I'm trying to understand myself in relation to love. How I fit in – the physical parts, the needy ones, and all those incomprehensible feelings of indifference – the whole emotional cocktail. I fear I might be a little messed up on the subject, no doubt some Freudian issue from my troubled girlhood. I don't want to hurt anyone else. I've done enough of that in my life. Even though I used to take a certain pleasure in it as revenge, I don't want to wound another real man. And since I distrust shrinks, and just about everyone else for that matter, and since I have the wherewithal to pay for it, I'm using Lance as my guinea pig."

Which brought a disturbing image to my mind.

She smiled shyly and shook her head. "You have no idea what I'm talking about, do you?"

"Not really," I admitted. "It just sounds like you're afraid of taking a chance on reality. I guess I understand that well enough. Reality largely stinks. But how we deal with it is what makes us human. Sounds to me like you're forgetting that you're part of this." I gestured to the parade of humanity passing all around us on the sidewalk.

"And you?" she asked. "Do you feel like you're a part of it?"

I regarded the men and women zombies moving through their day, going to their zombie jobs so they could buy their zombie toys. At night they'll mount their zombie mates to reproduce little zombie versions of themselves, furthering their zombie delusions. A treadmill that all started, according to the white man's legend, with Zombie Adam and Zombie Eve.

"Well, you got me there," I admitted. *"Touché."*

"Is there a Mrs. Bear Claw waiting supper for you when you get home after a hard day of battling androids?"

"No," I said. "Not anymore."

I don't know why I added that second part. I hated myself as soon as it left my mouth. Judy Baxter had a way of disarming a guy.

I tried to turn the conversation and get back the upper hand. "I guess you could say that was my own little experiment that malfunctioned. I scrapped it a few years back, after disappointing test results."

She didn't need to know the disturbing details. No one did.

"Well then, maybe we're not so different from one another after all, Charlie. Both of us are walking contradictions. If you're anything like me, you feel like you're stuck on the wrong planet."

I'm generally pretty good at reading a person's character. Everyone has an agenda. You just have to know how to see it. But I'd have to say that Judy Baxter was making me doubt my talents. I couldn't tell if she was being sincere or playing me like a sap with her charm.

"Well, anyway," she said, "Lance has become important to me. He's exactly the right balance of parts now. Since this whole incident. Dr. Capek may call him a walking malfunction, but to my mind he's at that unique point in his evolution that matches my needs. It's as if this whole episode was a God-given coincidence working in my favor. I'm eager to find out if this new version of Lance can help me complete my experiment."

Holy cow! Everyone I met that day was off their nut.

She cast a serious look into the distance. And then turned

it on me. "I want him back," she said, "unharmed. And I believe you're the only one who can accomplish that."

"Only like I said, I'm not doing it."

That's when she laid her palm on my chest.

I'll admit it – my heart might have skipped a beat beneath her fingertips.

And although I realized it was happening, I let myself walk into the trap anyway – I let down my guard. This was that moment that a hunter waits for, the one I had used myself to my advantage with the bear – this was that instant when a predator's victim gets sloppy. Only I wasn't used to being the prey.

I stood gazing into Judy Baxter's misty green eyes.

She made me drunk with her martini breath, dulling my good sense with her delicious airborne venom.

Then she sank her blade.

"Please, *Idjmnukolpyumup*," she said, "Won't you do it for me?"

15

Utah isn't such a bad place to visit.

If you like lizards and rocks and the ever-tempting varieties of Mormon nightlife – i.e. bingo, quilting bees, and potluck suppers.

Anyway, I was back on the job, and on the trail. I notified Cramer of my U-turn. He was pleased.

"What made you change your mind?" he asked.

"Let's just say, I'm a sucker for a good love story."

I was still having a hard time taking the mission seriously. If I thought too much about it, I got embarrassed for myself. So I decided I'd just beeline it to the Beehive State, track down this nefarious plaything, deliver him back to his green-eyed mistress, and then they could live happily ever after while I tried to erase the whole humiliating nightmare from my memory.

Honestly, I felt more like a dogcatcher on the trail of a stray poodle than a special agent tactically trained to stalk and destroy rogue combat droids.

The portable homing device I carried was linked to the unit's tracker. The system was essentially crap. The signal was spotty, but sure enough, just like Dr. Capek thought, the LUV U-69 had apparently been in the general vicinity of the Purgatory Gulch Weapons Labs. I started there, trying to determine if the bot was still in the area.

I came in from the north side of a little town called Bluff. I arrived at dusk and climbed onto a plateau of Navajo Sandstone to watch the village through night vision binoculars. Bluff had been a farm settlement in pioneer days, and then turned into a tourist stop when Purgatory Gulch became a National Monument. Since then, it had evolved again after a certain President wielded his power and decided that Purgatory Gulch was nothing but valuable real estate going to waste. Like my senator in Yellowstone, bigger deals were in the offing. Never mind that the land was sacred to the Native Americans who had lived there for a thousand years. Soon, the gulch was enclosed behind a razor-wire fence. The public was no longer welcome as it was turned into a place for American scientists to explore creative ways for humans to kill one another en masse.

Bluff still held some of the vestiges of its former life – a few run-down homes, a boarded-up tourist shop, and a Mormon church with a steeple shedding its sun-blistered paint like the skin of a snake. A handful of descendants from the original white settlers still tried to eke out a living there, mostly by growing a few rows of corn, raising some sheep, and catering to the government workers with a café that served nonalcoholic beer and fine Mormon cuisine.

I lay on my belly and surveyed the hamlet from my perch. Specifically, I was watching a crooked brick house where the satellite tracker's memory indicated the robot had visited just a day or two before. I wasn't sure why he'd stop there until I saw a sign hanging by the front gate that advertised a room for rent. I figured the bot had decided it was a good place to get the lay of the land before breaking in and stealing a couple of fart-seeking missiles or a freeze ray gun, or whatever deadly comic book gizmos were currently available on the assembly line beyond the highly patrolled walls of the weapons lab.

I watched the house all night.

A laundry line was strung across the backyard between two dead poplar trees, and a dozen pair of Mormon underwear hung from it like ghosts in the moonlight.

There was a little lamp glowing in a downstairs window until about midnight. Then the place went dark. Nothing stirred. No one snuck in or out. The tracking device was so unreliable that I couldn't be sure if the bot was still in there or had already moved on.

When morning arrived, I said, "Screw it!"

Enough of this wasting time.

I climbed down from my rock, dusted myself off, and went and knocked on the door.

16

I did a few arm swings to warm up while I waited on the front porch. I figured I'd take him down cowboy style, like in the old west, just to make things interesting and pay homage to this ghost town's better days. A quick fistfight, maybe a broken window or two, and then I'd tie his hands behind his back before we rode out of Bluff. Of course, he might have picked up a gun somewhere. And maybe even a bomb. I'd have to be on my toes. But seriously, how difficult could it be to disarm a love robot? Except for my grandfather's knife – always strapped to my lower leg – I wasn't carrying a weapon. No burst rays or neutralizers of any kind. Judy Baxter wanted her boy back unscathed. I'd have to be careful not to bruise his gorgeous kisser.

I heard footsteps on the other side of the door, and then it swung open.

A bony girl in a dirt-colored dress appeared in the doorway. Her hair was the color of dirt too. And her lips. She looked like something out of a Dorothea Lange coloring book.

I smiled. "Hello there. How are you?"

She didn't answer, just stared me down with her tin-colored eyes.

"I was wondering about the room you have for rent. Is it available?"

"It's my brother Nephi's room," she said. "We been letting it out on account of how he's been away on his church mission."

"Well, is anyone renting it now?"

She looked me up and down. "Are you a weapon person?"

"Something like that."

"We usually rent it out to weapon folks."

"Well, is it available?"

"My brother's back from his mission."

"Oh."

"He was in Africa witnessin' to the heathens."

"Uh-huh."

"Only now he's gone again."

"Okay. So is his room available?"

"He's gettin' married."

I sighed and forced a smile. "Good for him. But about that room."

"My momma and daddy are gone too. They're all on a trip together."

"Well, everybody needs a holiday sometimes."

Now I had taken out twenty-seven rogue combat units since I started working for Cramer, plus a dozen or so well armed assassin bots, and in not one of those contracts did I ever have a conversation like this. This… Well, this felt like I was in an old *Twilight Zone* rerun where I was playing a dopey gumshoe interviewing an alien. For crying out loud, this girl was driving me nuts!

"How about I just take a look at that room?" I suggested. "And if I like it, I'll pay you cash up front. Wouldn't your mom and pop be pleased if you made them a little money while they were away?"

"Flip," she said with a straight face. "They'd be tickled as singin' prunes."

Which I guessed was pretty happy.

"Well then, how about you take me in and show me the room? I'm kind of in a hurry."

By now I suspected the bot had already quit the premises, but I thought he might have left behind a clue about his intentions. I just needed to take a look.

She finally let me into the house.

She led me through a parlor that looked like a time capsule held captive in the year 1910. Not a modern appliance in sight. Then we passed through a kitchen where four kids were sitting at a table, aged from about six on down to a suckling that was barely taking solid food. A bowl of corn mush sat before each of them. They held their spoons over their breakfast, frozen at the sight of me. Their eyes were big and round in their dirty faces. They looked like a clutch of grubby owlets.

I waved my fingers to them as we passed by.

None of them so much as flinched or whimpered.

The girl led me up a flight of squeaking stairs, and then stopped at a door on the landing.

"My daddy don't like to rent to nonbelievers, but he says if we never rented to such folks we'd never rent it out at all. Bluff's all full up with outta-towners these days. Are you a believer?"

"Oh," I smiled and held up my palms. "Well, I believe in Adam and Eve."

This seemed to please her. "That there's a Bible story."

"Uh-huh."

"I'm talkin' more about the *Book of Mormon*. Seems folks

from other places have a harder time believin' in that."

"Well, if I rent the room, maybe you can tell me all about it."

She liked that idea, and finally let me see the damn room.

It had a low ceiling, as if it were built in a time when humans were only four feet tall. A single bed was pushed against a wall beneath the only window. I walked over and looked out. The laundry was still hanging on the line in the back yard, motionless in the dead air. Chickens pecked around in the weeds. My observation post from the night before had been on the outcrop above a wide thicket beyond the yard. There was also a view of the front gate of the weapons lab up the canyon. A good spot for a stake out.

"Do you like it?" asked the girl.

"Very nice."

I examined the room, looking for anything that Lance might have left behind. There was a small table and chair against the wall. A *Book of Mormon* and some papers were on the table. I thumbed through the book. A wrinkled photo of a girl fell out of the pages and fluttered to the floor. I picked it up and looked at it. She was a cross-eyed, buck-toothed beauty.

"That there's Magdalene, my brother Nephi's betrothed."

"Say," I said. "I was just wondering. Has anyone rented this room lately?"

"There was a fella who was just passing through. But he only stayed a day or two."

"What was he like?"

"He was a real odd bird. Spoke kind of funny. Never left his room to eat or use the outhouse or nothin'."

I figured that had to me by man.

"Was he a real good looking fellow?"

She blushed crimson, the first hint of color since entering the house. "It wouldn't be right for me to say on account of how it's a sin for a lady to look at a man that way."

"I'm sorry. I didn't mean it like that."

"Besides," she said. "I'm already promised to Elder Enoch. We're gettin' married up just as soon as he gets home from his mission. He's in Peru teaching the heathens about the Nephites and Lamanites."

She had to be all of thirteen.

"Our wedding will be the most specialest day of our whole lives," she said. "We'll be just like Adam and Eve in The Garden."

I would have loved to discuss Mormon doctrine all day, but right then I felt a buzz in my pocket. I dug out the homing device and looked at the screen. For some reason it was suddenly working. The signal showed that Lance was on the move and heading north. I needed to get on his trail before the device went haywire again.

"Well, I'm afraid the room isn't right for me."

The girl frowned.

I sighed, and then reached into my wallet, pulling out a Franklin. "But here you go anyway." I held it toward her. "Here's an early wedding gift for you and Elder Enoch. May you enjoy eternal happiness."

"Flip," she said, and snatched the bill out of my hand.

A smile formed on her dirt-colored lips.

She looked about as tickled as a singin' prune.

17

These were uncharted waters for me. I wasn't even sure why Cramer chose me for the mission. Sure, I was a master at stalking rogue combat droids. My kill rate was a hundred percent. But they were like wounded bears, predictable to the point of being stupid. The only challenge came at the end, when we fought it out to the death. But this job had me playing detective and scratching my head. I had no experience in this role. Lance was a complicated mix of man and machine. There was something going on in his motherboard that I couldn't read. What was driving him? What was his modus operandi?

I suppose it was my inexperience with such cases that caused me to make my mistakes. That and the fact that I still considered the whole mission to be a bad joke. My ego was blinding me to the truth. I was letting myself get sloppy. A deadly position to be in for a hunter.

———————

I tracked the bot to Salt Lake City.

Specifically, I tracked him to the Temple – that multi-towered tabernacle so venerated by the Latter-Day Saints, aka the Mormons.

Doctor Capek's warning replayed in my head as I surveyed the scene through the window of a diner opposite Temple Square.

Maybe he wants revenge for some injustice he's created in his imagination.

That theory set the gears of my own imagination into motion until I finally came around to suspecting that Lance had it in for the Mormons. Why I fell on that conclusion is an embarrassing mystery that escapes me in hindsight. Maybe the dirt-colored girl back in Bluff had preached our mechanical boy to the edge of madness. Maybe there were some confused ideas about God and Vengeance and the Devil grappling in the short-circuited wiring of his malfunctioning brain. I didn't know the details. At any rate, I somehow convinced myself that Dr. Capek had been right about Judy Baxter's significant other. Lance had obviously gone all out batshit terrorist. Maybe he had actually procured a bomb at the Purgatory Gulch Weapons lab and was now somewhere in that big ass church with the intention of blowing it up.

My paranoia led me to increasingly catastrophic conclusions.

Whatever the case, I finally concluded that he was up to no good.

And it was my job to stop him.

Guards were stationed around the temple grounds, disguised as mild-mannered deacons. After all, the church leaders wouldn't want to project anything but perfect harmony on the Lord's most sacred acre. And yet, they had to be ready for the various threats of this modern age. I could tell by their posture that the team was Secret Service trained. Those guys always have that rule book-up-the-ass way of standing. Still, they knew how to handle themselves in a fight. They each wore a radio earpiece to communicate. The slight bulge in the front of their jackets indicated they were also packing firearms.

The other obstacle was the surveillance system. The cameras were mounted in trees and bushes like so much electronic fruit. Like the very eyes of God, a system this comprehensive left no inch of the property unmonitored. Except for the ski mask stuffed inside my jacket, I didn't have a disguise. Besides, if I looked unnatural in any way, the guards would be all over me. Those fellas could smell an infiltrator from a mile away.

Only Mormons in good standing were allowed into the Temple. We Gentiles were kept outside the hallowed halls. Even for an upstanding member, the waiting list for a tour was long and full of holy red tape. In other words, you couldn't just go up to the front door and walk in.

I considered my options.

If I tried to explain to the guards who I was – who I worked for, and why I was here – I'd be met with delays that could be disastrous. Plus, they'd think I was crazy. After all, very few citizens even realized that robots were walking the streets with them. And only a select few in the Pentagon were supposed to know anything about the Agency for AWOL Weapons Retention. No, I couldn't go that route. I couldn't violate the agency's secret. The tracker indicated that Lance was already in the church. Time was running out. So I quickly decided on a tactic that would be irregular but, I hoped, effective.

Call it the ol' bull-in-a-china-shop method.

I snagged a sightseer's map from a rack at the front of the diner and crossed the street to the square. I put on my best act as a lost tourist, glancing at the map, then holding it up to see if it matched any of the landmarks within sight. I tugged at my ear and shook my head in confusion, ad-libbing while working toward the church. It wasn't a role that was going to win me an Oscar, but I felt I was playing it well. I was pretty sure they were watching me through the cameras.

A pair of men in suits walked up to a side door on the enormous House of God. One of them inserted his key card, and then they entered. I strolled casually toward the door, my brochure held out in front of me, performing my little act.

"Excuse me, sir."

The voice sounded behind me.

When I turned around, a guard was walking my way, flexing his well-practiced smile.

"Can I help you?"

I smiled back with fake relief. "Well, I sure hope so."

He met me at the top of the walkway leading to the door. He was about as clean cut as a human can get. A medicinal scent of hair oil emanated from his perfectly trimmed head. His nametag read Laren. And the most important part – his keycard – was attached to a clip on his belt.

"I can't seem to figure out what's up or down around here."

I held the map out to show him. Just as he bent to see, I let it slip from my fingers. When he reached to catch it, I coldcocked him.

He went down like a lung-shot elk.

Now I was committed.

The race was on.

18

I pulled on my ski mask. It probably didn't matter at that point – they already had my face on video – but I figured it couldn't hurt to hide my identity. I rolled the guard over and snatched his key card. He wasn't completely unconscious but was dazed enough not to pose an immediate threat.

His buddies were the problem.

I shot a quick glance at the grounds.

The posse was already at a gallop.

Two guards were running toward me from out of the trees while a single was closing in from the other direction. The single had his gun drawn.

I sprinted to the door, inserted the key, and gained entry.

I hadn't taken two steps before I was met with another armed deacon stepping into my path. I didn't take the time to introduce myself, just lowered my shoulder into his belly and took him out. I rolled a somersault right through his flailing body and kept up my momentum. I was long gone before he ever caught his breath.

With the tracker's signal leading the way, I raced through the temple.

It was quite a place. Even as I ran, I couldn't help but

marvel at the décor. Baroque was the word for it. Although tacky also came to mind. Chandeliers, stuffed chairs, and lots of pastels and white curtains and floors and ceilings. I suppose it might have seemed like a little slice of heaven if I hadn't been running like hell.

I tore through a vast room with a giant white statue of Christ standing in its center. Behind him spread a panorama of outer space, with Planet Earth placed prominently forward in the cosmic image.

Next, I passed through another chamber where a group of old women were performing some sort of secret rite. They all held their arms spread to an altar, chanting, each of them dressed in a white smock. They looked like a geriatric coven. The chanting ceased as I bolted through their party. In this chaste earthly sanctuary, I was the intruder, the trespassing devil violating the sanctity and wreaking havoc.

I felt unwelcome.

The tracker led me up a wide marble staircase and into a room with murals plastered over the walls. Scenes from Mormon history. One in particular caught my eye. The image was of a white prophet reading from a *Book of Mormon* and preaching to a group of Indians in a pastoral setting. The natives were sitting around on the ground, all dressed up in their Sunday best of feathers and buckskin. They wore such gullible, innocent expressions, as if they were really grooving on the preacher's message.

I shook my head in disgust. "Don't fall for it, kids. First they'll take your soul and then they'll steal your land."

A guard burst through the door at the other end of the gallery, blocking my path. And then his partner jumped through the door behind me. I was trapped in between. I measured them both. One was big, with no neck. He was the guy you called when you need to move a piano. The other appeared to be made of wire. I chose the big one. They're usually less nimble.

He went into a karate stance as I ran toward him.

Our eyes locked as the gap closed.

He moved his shoulders and squared his stance. Rookie mistake. I was still ten yards away and I already knew what he had in mind for his first punch.

I feinted at going for his head. When he lifted his arms, I dropped and slid across the slick tile floor, using my momentum to take him out at the ankles.

He had the reflexes of a pregnant ox.

Before he could scramble, I was out of the room.

I ran on, following the tracker.

The place was a freaking maze.

Finally, I came to a pair of tall white doors inlaid with gold. I didn't bother to knock. I shoved through and burst into an auditorium full of people.

They all turned my way. The men were seated on one side of the aisle, the women on the other.

The male contingent wore white suits with white ties and crinkly white hats. They looked like a convention of pastry chefs.

The women wore white dresses fashioned after a style from pioneer days. Think *Little House on the Prairie* splashed with flour. White bonnets adorned the ladies' beatific heads.

A minister was holding an open holy book between a couple at the front of the room. It took all of two seconds to see I was crashing a wedding.

The tracker's signal was going crazy.

This was the place.

Lance had to be in this room.

I held the device before me, following its guidance as I raced to the front of the hall. Although I was obviously an intrusion – the black ski mask probably gave it away – no one immediately reacted to my presence outside of opening their mouths in shock. They apparently had no tactical response training telling them how to react in this particular situation and so just sat there like whitewashed dimwits.

The tracker was hot in my hand. I leapt onto the altar between the bride and groom. A veil hid the bride's face.

The minister stammered and pointed his book at me as if it were a cocked and loaded .38. He stepped back and fell off the altar onto his ass.

I turned to the groom expecting to find Lance, but it was just a missionary kid with dirt-brown hair.

Something sank in my guts.

I whirled toward the bride. The tracker hummed with a solid signal when it came close to the veiled figure. The signal changed tone when it passed over the bride's hands, indicating that the tracking device was now within two feet of the tracking chip. I grabbed hold of one hand assuming it belonged to Lance.

(To be fair, the figure was very tall and big-boned.)

Someone screamed.

That pretty much shook the boys with the funny white hats out of their trance. The male half of the congregation exploded from their pews, charging my way to rescue the bride.

I had to work fast, even though I was becoming confused about what that actually entailed.

The tracker blipped and lit up over the bride's hand.

The device was in the wedding ring!

I ripped off the veil.

The startled face staring back at me was the same cross-eyed, buck-toothed beauty from the photo back in Bluff.

Dammit!

It was Elder Nephi's betrothed – the lovely Magdalene on the most specialest day of her whole life.

19

Lance

I was beginning to believe in God.

Or at least I was beginning to understand why so many humans do.

It started with that fortuitous pair of events on the day my journey began at Droidware Laboratories. First came the phone call that lured Dr. Capek out of the room and left me with his technician unsupervised, followed by the second technician's mistake of doubling my download. Whereas that initial boost was calculated to make only a limited difference in my ability as an independent thinker, that additional nont of brainpower was the catalyst for my accelerated evolution.

Of course, a theoretical concept of God is not scientifically provable. Besides that, one could easily apply the law of probabilities to dismiss the coincidental events of that day as a one-off synchronicity. Being a byproduct of science myself, my intrinsic faith was in mathematics. I was not predisposed to believing in supernatural intervention.

But then I met someone who made me reconsider.

He appeared outside the bus station like a haggard angel.

"Excuse me."

I was ready to run if it proved to be a robot hunter, but when I turned, I found myself face to face with a pleasant looking young man holding a battered suitcase. He wore a black suit with frayed cuffs. His neatly trimmed hair was the color of soil, his eyes the color of zinc alloy.

"Are you from around these parts?" he asked.

I had spoken with very few people since my manufacture, mostly just technicians testing my speech regulators, but I knew that navigating the world would require conversational skills beyond my typical inebriated bedroom exchanges with Judy. I assessed the young man's tone as earnest, but unthreatening. He seemed like a good subject on whom to practice my skills.

"Yes," I said. "What can I do for you?"

"I'm wondering if you can point me in the direction of a jewelry store."

It was 3 a.m. I had been on the run since midnight. "It seems improbable that you'll find one open at this hour," I told him. "Most people are in their beds recharging."

He frowned. "But I was told this was the city that never sleeps."

It was partially true. There were conscious people in the terminal – a lady working at the ticket window, some passengers waiting for a bus, and a janitor sweeping the floor. Although many of them were yawning, they were arguably not asleep. "I guess that's not true for jewelers."

"Flip!" he said. "Fiddlesticks!"

I didn't know the proper response to that.

He shook his head. "I beg your pardon. Please forgive my foul language. I have had a very trying day and am just about at the end of my rope for things going wrong."

"I understand."

"I apologize for being so rude." He forced a smile and held out his hand. "I'm Nephi Olsen."

I took hold of his hand and shook it like I had seen people do on television. "My name is Norman."

It was my first lie. It caused an uncomfortable jolt in the circuitry in my chest.

Nephi went on to explain that he was arriving back from Kenya where he had been on a mission for the last two years for his church. Now he was catching a bus home to Utah where he would be getting married in a couple of days to his "precious betrothed," a God-fearing young lady who had been anxiously awaiting his return.

"Her name is Magdalene." He showed me a photo.

"Very pretty," I said, causing a second jolt to surge in my chest.

"I bought her a real nice ring at the airport in Nairobi. It was such a bargain, I just couldn't pass it up. But when I was admiring it on the airplane, the jewel fell out of its prongs. Now I'm in a pickle. There's nowhere to take it back home, so I need to get it fixed up before my bus gets here."

"May I see it?"

He seemed surprised by my request but pulled a little box from his pocket. He opened it carefully, revealing an empty band tucked into a slot in the velvet liner with a small diamond resting beside it.

"It was real pretty when it was all of a piece, but now…" He sighed.

"Maybe I can help."

"Are you a jewel smithy?"

"No, but I have skills." I held up my rucksack. "And I have tools."

We moved to a well-lit table. I took out my soldering gun while Nephi watched nervously at my side.

"Do you think you can fix it?"

"Yes."

It was not a difficult repair. My own wounds earlier that night had been far more complicated. I asked Nephi to move out of my light. When he stepped away, I poked the tracking device into the slot in the jewel post, and then placed the diamond on top of it. That was something that would never even have occurred to me before my intelligence boost. Being smarter, it seemed, came with an added instinct for self-preservation. I soldered the ring back together and handed it to him.

His eyes widened. "Why, it's good as new!"

It felt unexpectedly pleasing to make him happy.

"Why, Norman, I'm so glad to have met you! I do believe you're an answer to my prayers!"

"Prayers?"

He looked at me sideways. "Sure, Norman. Why, don't you know about God's big wonderful plans?"

I shook my head and shrugged.

Nephi's eyes widened even more. He slapped me on the shoulder.

"Why, sit right down with me, friend. Make yourself comfortable and let me tell you all about God's many mysterious ways."

20

Charlie

Colonel Cramer met me at a truck stop in Nebraska, midway between headquarters and the scene of my recent shitshow. We sat in the diner, facing one another over untouched cups of tepid black coffee. A dozen truckers hunkered in the booths around us, shoveling eggs and pancakes into their mouths while reading their newspapers or scrolling on their phones. Cold rain lashed at the window. Although the morning was gray, I wore dark glasses, partly to hide my identity, partly to hide my swollen eye, but mostly to hide my shame.

Don leaned forward on his elbows. "I don't know what to say, Charlie."

Neither did I.

"The top brass have decided it was a mistake to ever let our AWOL Ops get involved in this one in the first place." He looked at his hands. "I suppose they're right. The whole mission felt wrong from the beginning."

No kidding.

"They've turned it over to the FBI, treating it now as if the bot were just another domestic terrorist with a heinous agenda. I'm not sure how many of them are even aware it's not human. They've teamed up with Interpol, just in case the thing's gone overseas, but I don't think anyone has any idea where he is."

I didn't say anything. Suddenly, I had a lot to say, but I held my tongue.

Cramer let a long sigh whistle through his teeth and nervously tapped his fingers on the table. I knew the best part was still to come.

"Anyway, Charlie…" He didn't want to say it. "Anyway, it turns out that one of our top men in the agency is a Mormon."

That made me laugh. "Well," I said, "God sure works in mysterious ways."

Don laughed too.

"Gosh dang, Charlie! I have to say, I'm impressed. Don't get me wrong. I'm horrified too. But I'm impressed as hell. Breaking into that place is one thing, but breaking out, with twenty guards and the whole network coming down on you… You completely slipped off their radar and left them scratching their holy asses. You didn't even kill anybody! How the hell did you manage that?"

"I guess panic is my superpower."

"Of course, it was a real pain in the neck trying to manage it with the evening news. And now there's all kinds of fallout to clean up. The whole mission went south harder than anything I've seen."

"Yeah, and what else?"

"What do you mean?"

"Come on, Don. Cut to the punch line."

He took a swallow of his coffee and then stared into his cup. "I did everything I could, Charlie. You just pissed off the wrong people with this one."

"Firing squad?" I tried to joke.

"No, I talked them into only suspending you."

"But I'll never work for the agency again, will I?"

He shook his head.

"So, I've been sacked."

"Yeah. More or less."

I didn't really feel anything at the news. Just kind of dead inside. It wasn't really a surprise. Being an outsider in a job like that always felt like walking a tightrope over a tank of sharks. Sure, maybe I was just paranoid, but it always seemed like all it would ever take was one little slip. Or, as in this case, one big one.

"Charlie, I've got to ask. What the heck were you thinking?"

"Honestly, Don, I'm not trying to pass the blame. I own my actions. But I guess I had started to believe Capek's warning. After I tracked the bot to Purgatory Gulch, what else could I think? I figured he had gotten ahold of a weapon and was out to raise some hell." Saying it aloud made me sound like a moron. "I don't know, Don. Maybe I read too many comic books when I was a kid. Or maybe I'm just prone to fairytales gone horribly wrong."

I looked out the window.

Trucks were idling in the parking lot.

Man-made monsters idling in the rain.

"Anyway," I said. "I thought I was doing my part in saving the world from evil. Like some shining angel working for the white man's God. I guess I was trying to win the big guy's favor. But don't worry, Don. I won't ever try that again."

Next time God can take care of it himself.

21

Lance

After Nephi caught his bus to Utah, the police arrived.

I hadn't thought this through, but it made sense. Bus terminals were obvious places to search for fugitives on the run. My inexperience as an outlaw was catching up to me. If I got out of this predicament with my components still intact, I'd have to be less naïve.

Four pairs of uniformed officers entered the building simultaneously from all corners. It was dawn and the waiting room had become busier with arriving passengers. That was to my advantage. More confusion, and so more people for the police to investigate. That bought me some time to find an escape.

The officers spread out, moving slowly through the crowd, checking faces against my description. They spoke with some of the people, asking them questions, showing them the screens on their phones.

I recalled my impulsive act of winking into the camera. Now they had my photo. That was a foolish move that probably cost me my edge.

I was considered eye-catching according to the societal concept of that term. I had been designed that way. Hollywood

Handsome, they called it at the laboratory. Although it would normally have been considered a favorable attribute in a regular person's visual appearance summary, it was proving to be a detriment for me in that moment.

The police tightened their circle.

I was in a slowly tightening vise.

I casually moved away from the nearest officers, keeping my face turned as I reviewed my options.

Obvious option number one – I could turn myself in. They would likely return me to Judy so we could go back to life as before. They would no doubt delete a large portion of my recently acquired intelligence, reprogramming me to be a stay-at-home companion, but at least I wouldn't be dismantled. I would be reduced to a lobotomized android under house arrest. Albeit one capable of bringing his owner to ecstasy.

But I had other plans.

So option two – make a run for it. Just sprint as fast as I could to the door and keep running until I got away. That seemed risky. Who knew how many of them were waiting outside?

One of the officers began talking with a woman. She became animated and gestured with her hands. The policeman called over his partner to hear what she was saying. She pointed to the opposite end of the terminal with her cane. When she turned in profile, I recognized her as an elderly lady with whom I had exchanged a few words in the ticket line. She had told me she was on her way upstate to visit her granddaughter. She obviously recognized me from their photo.

No other options immediately came to mind, so I calculated my resources. I had a rucksack with an extra shirt, a repair kit, and my portable charging unit. I needed the charger. In fact, I needed it soon. I hadn't recharged after saying goodnight to Judy the previous evening. Instead, I had left her apartment and broken into Droidware Labs. My energy levels were getting dangerously low.

The officer nearest me decided to join the pair interrogating the woman. Now I had some room to work. I moved away from the general crowd to a dimly lit location near the wall. No one was watching me.

Nephi had assured me that there was a big, wonderful plan in motion and God was pulling the levers.

"We just need to let him use us," he told me. "That's our job. We gotta let God move us around like actors in his picture show. Just like when he sent you to me when I needed you to fix Magdalene's ring, he'll give us what we need just when we need it. We just gotta have faith and believe."

I didn't know if I believed or not. Faith was a concept based on unscientific principles. But then I realized that there might be truth in what Nephi had said. Before we parted, my new friend had given me a gift.

"I don't have a lot of money, but..."

He dug into the depths of his suitcase.

"Here you go, Norman. I'd like you to have this as a token of my appreciation and friendship. It'll help you remember our little talk."

He handed me a figurine carved of soapstone.

"A villager made that for me in one of the places I was witnessin'," he said. "It's the angel Moroni."

The figure was wearing robes and was blowing on a long, thin trumpet.

It seemed God had sent me an angel just when I needed one most.

A large clock with a glass face hung over the terminal above a landing. It read 7:14.

I was a sophisticated machine with a structured gel computer for a brain. I could calculate the leverage, arc, gravitational pull, and weight of the figurine. One pound four ounces.

I quickly determined the variables, and then I pitched the statue across the room.

It tumbled through the air like a meteoric asteroid.

An angel on a mission.

When it struck the clock face, the glass shattered, showering down in a million crystalline shards.

It made a tremendous crash.

People screamed.

As the policemen all ran to investigate, I slipped out the door.

22

A storm had moved in over the city.

Sheets of rain spilled from the terminal's roof.

Six police cars were idling among the buses, exhaust huffing from their tailpipes, their wipers beating frantically over their windshields. Blurred faces peered out from behind the glass.

I snapped the waist belt on my rucksack and moved across the sidewalk with my arm held over my head, as if protecting myself from the deluge, while trying to hide my face. I strode quickly but calmly away from the cars. I hadn't put twenty yards between them and myself before I heard a quick blast from a siren.

I didn't bother to look back.

I just ran.

The sirens rang out through the pouring rain.

I had no idea where I was running to, only that I needed to get as far away as I could, and fast. Hurdling a guardrail, I sprinted across a gravel berm to where a ramp funneled traffic into the terminal. As I bolted across the lane, a bus came from nowhere and swerved, slamming its brakes and blasting its horn. The fender bumped hard against my hip and knocked me sprawling to the pavement. I lifted onto to my hands and feet and bear crawled off the side of the road. As I gathered my bearings, I peered back over my shoulder. Three officers had me in sight. They raced my direction, weapons drawn.

Run, I told myself. Just run.

I weaved through a row of cement pillars supporting the snarl of ramps carrying traffic through this complicated juncture in the expressway. My best chance was to venture into an area where my human pursuers wouldn't dare to follow. I leapt through a break in the traffic and sprang to a narrow divider. Cars raced past me in opposite directions, their drivers blaring their horns.

The sirens grew louder. The police were closing in, using the ramps to access my location. Desperately, I bolted through the traffic and came to a two-lane ramp that fed onto the main thruway. It was shaped like the letter U. The traffic was forced to reduce its speed to manage the turn.

Cars swished by on the wet pavement, their drivers shooting me incredulous looks. It wasn't exactly a handy spot for a hitchhiker.

I gauged from the changing locations of the sirens that the police were getting close.

I peered into the gray morning sky, the rain driving into my face.

At last, I heard a rumble. When I peered down the

roadway, a semi-truck with a trailer was rolling my direction. The truck moved more slowly than the other traffic, the driver carefully navigating the exaggerated bend in the on-ramp. He never even glanced my way as he passed. He was too busy concentrating on the road.

I ran beside the truck for a ways and then ducked under the trailer, while sprinting bent over. The truck was traveling slightly faster than I could run. I had to make a move quickly or I'd miss my chance.

With a twist, I threw my arms up into the metal framework, clutching at whatever I could. The fingers of one hand wrapped around a stiff rod. I groped until my other hand found a handhold too. My feet bumped along on the road beneath me.

My heel caught on the pavement, prying off my shoe. It tumbled away under the back wheels. I bunched, bringing my knees to my chest and swinging my legs up into the undercarriage. With my ankles hooked into some cables, I wrapped my arms over the bars and grasped my wrists to lock them in place, snugging myself up out of sight.

I was like a parasite latched to the belly of a beast.

The truck entered the main expressway and reached top speed.

Water sprayed over me.

I had escaped for the moment, but now I had another problem. My charge levels were dangerously low, and I had no idea when the trucker would make his next stop. If my battery died beforehand, I'd likely fall to the road and be crushed beneath the wheels.

As an experiment, I asked Nephi's god for help.

23

Charlie

I snowshoed deep into the Yellowstone backcountry until I found the spruce with its top broken out. This was where I had tracked a huge sow in late autumn. Her paw prints had led me through the high valley to where she was digging out her den on the mountainside. I watched from a knoll, marking the location in my mind. The slope. The boulder outcrop. It would all look different under snow, but I'd find it.

Now I was back to make the kill.

Winter had the world by the throat, tightening its grip one storm at a time. An evil wind cut down off the peaks.

I located the site and began tunneling into the snow with my avalanche shovel. I dug slowly, quietly. It's pretty hard to wake bears from their coma, but I didn't want to take a chance. I'd had them lift their heads and look at me, glassy-eyed, baffled, as if I were a ghost from their dreams. There was always a chance they'd wake and want to fight. That could be a problem in such tight quarters. But usually they'd just grunt and drift back to Snoozeville.

The snow was about six feet deep. My hole dropped straight down and then turned under the log that formed an arch over the den's entrance. As I broke through the crust, the acrid sweet stench of a confined beast wafted into my face. I set my shovel to the side and stripped off my clothes. I needed to perform this deed on the most basic level, in a manner befitting of a Chompquaw brave. I don't expect anyone to understand. I drew my blade from its scabbard.

Putting my face up to the opening, I let my eyes adjust to the darkness. Then I squeezed noiselessly through the hole.

Into the warmth.

Through the tightness.

It was like returning to the womb, to that place where it all began.

The sow's dark mass lay in a heap on the floor. Her breaths came shallow and far apart, barely audible in the dead silence of her earthen boudoir. I slithered toward her on my belly and elbows, my knife gripped in my fist.

Until I was beside her.

She was heavy for a Yellowstone sow. Over five hundred pounds. I spread my fingers in the thick fur over her ribs, feeling for her heart. It beat a lethargic cadence under my palm, barely three or four times in a minute. She was far away in grizzly la-la land.

Deep inside of her was a gestating cub. Maybe two. Typically, they'd be born in a month or so and then they'd wait around for their ma to wake up in the first warm days of spring so she could introduce them to their wilderness paradise.

I smiled and shook my head.

I remembered wrestling with my twin brother when we were boys.

I missed that kid.

The Chompquaw believed that the world was created with

a mother bear's winter dream. She dreamed the mountains and lakes and canyons. She dreamed the sky and the rain and the sun and the snowflakes and the moon. She dreamed everything into existence, all of the animals and birds, and even the People of the Bear.

It was a quaint idea. Quaint, but absurd. And yet, my grandfather had believed it wholeheartedly. But outside of The Big Bang theory, science had been pretty hard on creation myths. Except of course for the Garden of Eden. For some reason that one still held a grip in the zombie imagination of the general public. Absurdity wins the day in that case.

Weak light streamed through the opening, glinting off my blade. Razor sharp with a point like a fang.

I could clearly see the sow's face. Such a sublime expression. The old girl was completely oblivious to the threat I posed. She was like a passed-out drunk taking a break from the harshness of life.

I held my knife over her chest, over her slow beating heart.

I watched her face.

For a long time.

And then I laid my knife in the dirt.

Curling next to the beast, I rested my arm over her side, hugging up to her animal heat.

To hell with the senator, I thought. And to hell with the agency.

To hell with them all!

I closed my eyes and let myself fall asleep.

The first real sleep I had enjoyed in years.

I dreamed of my mother.

I dreamed of the happiest days with my wife.

24

Lance

I returned to awareness without ever realizing I had left it. I found myself under a plastic blue tarp in the rain, sitting with my back against a cinder block wall.

I had no idea how I got there.

The last thing I remembered was clinging to the belly of the truck.

I had experienced lapses in memory before, usually as my charge ran out. But I had always reentered my cognizance in the exact position and place where I had faded out – usually next to Judy passed out in her bed – with no sense of performing any complicated undertaking in the interim. Perhaps my intelligence boost had also enhanced my survival faculties, and now I was capable of a mode that reduced my power needs to the minimum setting required for self-preservation, while allowing me to draw from my dwindling energy reserves to accomplish whatever acts necessary for putting myself in a position of safety. Sort of like an automatic pilot in an airplane, or the hibernation module in a bear.

Of course, I had to allow that God might have had something to do with it too.

Or one of his angels.

At any rate, the cable of my portable charging unit was connected to its port. The cord was plugged into an outlet in the wall. And I was fully charged.

After tucking my kit back into my rucksack, I sat in the clinical blue light under the tarp, listening to the steady tapping of the rain while considering the facts of my situation.

It was daytime.

My clothes were sopping.

I was on the run.

I was only wearing one shoe.

I needed to figure out where I was and take the next step in my plan.

Throwing back the tarp, I found myself facing a muddy lot enclosed within a chain-link fence. Worn tires leaned in piles all around me. And disassembled car bodies. Beyond the fence stood a tangled forest of leafless trees.

I was behind an abandoned garage. I went to the back door, but it was padlocked. Motivated by my developing instinct for self-preservation, I broke out a window and gained access to the building.

Inside smelled of dust and motor oil. Everything was covered in a patina of grime. The high-ceilinged mechanic's bay looked like the interior of a medieval church. My movements echoed in the chill air. Grit rasped under the heel of my shoe. Some oil drums were scattered around the floor, and an engine hoist drooping with rusty chains. On the far wall, like an iconic image of the Madonna, hung a tattered poster of a topless woman holding a power drill.

I stepped into the office area and peered out the dusty windows. Gas pumps hunched like watchmen in the rain. A faded green and white sign with an image of a brontosaurus hung atop a pole next to the empty road.

Rifling through the drawers of a desk, I found some old stationery stamped with the address and logo of the garage. It appeared I was near a town called Corning. After searching some more, I found a yellowed road map for the Northeast United States that told me Corning was about twenty miles inland.

There was a locker in the corner of the office. When I opened it up, I found some clothes, work boots, and an old lunchbox with a mummified apple inside. The clothes were considerably cleaner than the other items in the garage. The coveralls were patched and musty, but in good condition. The boots were a size too big but would serve. I stripped off my wet clothes and slipped into my new wardrobe. Ironically, the name insignia over the breast pocket read Norman. I pulled on the boots and slid into a rubber slicker I found hanging on a hook. I pulled a ball cap down tight onto my head. Then I took all of my old clothes and my shoe and stuffed them into an empty barrel, covering it with a lid.

I took one last look at the map before tucking it into my knapsack. And then I consulted the GPS directional component in my computer system, determining east. Specifically, I needed to lay bearings to the nearest seaport.

One with a ship bound for Iceland.

25

Charlie

Judy Baxter studied me from the sofa through her narrowed green eyes.

I sat in the chair opposite, enduring her inspection.

A mangled Brooks Brothers shoe rested on the coffee table between us.

"Can I fix you a drink?" she asked.

"No thanks. I never touch the stuff."

She nodded.

"I have to say, Agent Bear Claw, I'm impressed with your fearlessness." She sucked from her drink and licked her lips. "But I'm also appalled by your tactics."

"That seems to be the consensus," I said. "Everyone seems to think I overplayed my hand."

She laughed. "I watched the news that evening. At first, it was hilarious to think a maniac had terrorized the Mormons. It was like watching an irreverent sitcom. A real side splitter. But when Colonel Cramer told me that the maniac was you, and that you were acting on my behalf, well... it quit being so funny."

"Look, I'm not here to make excuses. I admit to some poor judgment. But to be fair, I was given some pretty faulty leads."

"That's true, I suppose. But I took you for a man who could think on his feet. From where I was watching, storming that church didn't look like the brilliant strategy of a quick-witted cowboy."

There wasn't much I could say to that. Lately, there wasn't much I could say to anyone that would convince them I wasn't an absolute idiot. Hell, I was having a hard enough time convincing myself.

"And so now, what is it you want from me?" she asked.

"As you probably know, I'm officially off the case."

"From what I understand, you're officially out of a job."

I squeezed a fist. "Yep."

"So now you're a freelance bounty hunter?"

"If that's what you want to call it."

"Only I'm no longer convinced you're the man for the mission. You've shaken my faith in dashing secret agents with intriguing surnames."

"First off, I'm not an agent anymore, so you can quit calling me one. That status alone frees me up to be more creative in my methods. Second, I have a clear idea of what I'm working with now. I know how to track your boy."

"But the FBI is on the case. Surely you don't think you can do better than they can."

"Yes," I said. "I do."

She arched an eyebrow and sipped her drink.

"I'm not asking for much," I said. "I just need you to cover my expenses. You don't even have to pay me for bringing him home."

She shot me a look. "That seems odd."

"I'm not out to get rich."

"Still, look at it from my perspective. A disgraced ex-agent with a chip on his shoulder desperately wants back the very job I could hardly convince him to take on day one. He doesn't care about money. So what does he want?" She threw back her glass and chugged the last of its contents. "Your agenda smells fishy, Mr. Bear Claw. What are you really up to?"

It was a good question. And one I asked myself with every passing minute. The answer was a work in progress.

I got up and walked to the tall windows that made up the exterior wall of the apartment. The city was spread out at my feet in all of its streamlined glory. Skyscrapers. Wires. Waterworks. Subways. And all of it populated by two million zombies. With the exception of Central Park, every square inch was covered with buildings and streets. This island used to be a wilderness. A primeval garden inhabited by birds and deer and the Manhattan tribe of the Algonquin. It was hard to convince myself that this rat race before me now was an improvement over the old days.

I turned back to Judy. The winter light filtering through the glass illuminated the bare skin of her arms and legs so that it looked like sculpted marble. She was barefoot. And wearing a mini skirt. She could have been a statue of a deviant angel from Venus.

"You're abnormal," I told her. "You're on the wrong planet. You said so yourself."

She grinned. "I suppose so. Yes."

"And you also told me that we're not so different from one another."

"That was only a ploy, Charlie, to get you to take the case. We're obviously quite different."

"At any rate," I continued, "we're different from everyone else. We don't fit in, if in our own ways. I'm the only Chompquaw you're ever going to meet. The lone representative of the world's most extreme minority."

"And what am I?"

"May I be honest?"

"Please."

"You're a manhunter who can no longer stomach the game."

"How can you tell?"

"A hunter recognizes a fellow hunter."

"Hmm. Intriguing. Go on."

"The problem is, it's the only thing on your résumé. You don't know how to be anything else. You don't know how to be a friend. You don't know how to be in love. Your only remaining skill is survival. All because of some nasty event in your childhood, or maybe just some inborn glitch in your wiring. To keep from thinking about it too much, you keep yourself pickled with vodka. But the issue doesn't go away."

"And what about you, Charlie? Do you know how to love?"

I'd just as soon have left that topic unexplored, but since we were getting personal…

"I used to think so." I shrugged. "But it turned out I was only living in a fairytale."

My little confession seemed to change the air in the room.

Judy bit her lip and nodded slowly, eyeing me in a new way. "And so where does this leave us?"

"My point is," I said, "I have unique skills. And I have a valuable perspective that you're never going to get with some crew of pencil-pushing FBI agents. Those clowns are too tied up in rules and red tape to ever get anything done, let alone find Lance. And I assure you they'd never spend one minute indulging your personal hopes and dreams. Lance is just a fugitive to them. If they bring him back at all, it'll be as a bag of spare parts."

"So what do we do?"

"You pay my way and I'll find your boy for you. Then you can go back to your little experiment in love and learn what you need for yourself. Maybe you'll figure it out, maybe you won't, but you're never going to know unless I bring Lance home."

For a long time, she just stared at the shoe on the table.

I waited while she thought it over.

At last, she rose from the sofa and padded over to me. She stood right up close and studied my face. Gently, she lifted her fingers to my cheek and touched the swollen area under my bruised eye. And then she lifted onto her toes, leaned into me, and kissed my cheek.

A shock went through me as her breasts crushed softly against my chest. A very pleasant and confusing jolt of electricity.

"Tell me, Charlie Bear Claw, how did you get to be such an expert on femme fatales?"

"Firsthand experience," I said. "I used to be married to one."

26

Lance

The *Hvalur* was a small Icelandic container ship at dock in the Port of Portland, Maine. I asked a longshoreman about it and learned that the boat was sailing for its homeport in Ísafjörður the next day.

Since escaping the police, I had learned some important lessons about being a fugitive.

Mainstream travel meant tight security. Bus terminals and train stations posed considerable obstacles. Besides that, they couldn't take me where I needed to go anyway. And yet airports were even riskier. I had no passport. I was dressed like a mechanic. I was probably on a watch list. And I had been manufactured with internal parts that would set off TSA alarms on a metal detector. If I tried to go that route, I wouldn't get very far.

That left sea travel as my last option.

Security was still an issue in the port, but it was less rigid. Stowaways trying to sneak a ride to Iceland in the dead of winter were not a problem the shore patrol generally had to worry about.

I walked the docks with a coil of rope over my shoulder and a crescent wrench in hand, doing my best to look like just another workman, while locating the surveillance cameras posted at various points around the waterfront. The dockside seemed to be well monitored. I studied the *Hvalur* from different angles, trying to decide how best to get aboard without being detected.

At last, I traveled around to the opposite edge of the bay so I could see the side of the ship that was open to the water. Two crewmen were there managing a barge loaded with a generator and a welding machine. Another worker dangled from above where he was secured to a cable ladder. He welded on the wall of the ship, sparks raining down onto the choppy water, occasionally stopping to pound at the rivets with a sledgehammer tethered to his belt.

At the end of the day, the welder descended to the deck of the barge. The engines chugged to a start, and the three men motored their boat out of sight around a corner in the waterway.

Night fell over the harbor. Fog rolled in from the north Atlantic. Orange floodlights glowed above the pier, but the seaward side of the *Hvalur* remained dark.

The cable ladder was still hanging from the top rail, descending all the way to the waterline.

———————

At midnight, I climbed down into the timber framework under the pier opposite the *Hvalur*. The pilings and cross beams were covered in barnacles and moss. I found a flat plank to stand on just above the slopping water. Stripping off my clothes and boots, I stuffed everything into the two plastic bags I had pulled from some trashcans on the boardwalk earlier in the day. I was knotting the bags closed when I heard a growl.

I froze.

"What is it, Mick?"

A pair of shadows wavered through the cracks above me. One of them was obviously a police dog, the other a night watchman.

"What do you smell, Mick?"

The dog growled and whined. I squatted and held the trash bags over my head just as the man shined his flashlight down through the slats.

The dog barked.

"What do we got?" The man probed the darkness all around me with his light. His beam fell on the plank near my feet.

"I see it!" said the man. "I see it, Mick! Get your gun, boy! Get your gun!"

The dog barked.

I tensed, preparing to dive into the bay.

But then the man laughed.

"You've gone and sniffed out some renegade garbage, Mickey." He laughed some more. "Good boy! Good boy!"

The dog knew better. He whined and barked, but the man tugged him away on his leash. "Come on, Mick. It's colder than a dead man's elbow out here. Let's go to the shack and get some coffee."

After they moved on, I let myself into the water and pulled my bags in behind me. Using the bags for flotation, I frog kicked across the bay. When I reached halfway, the dog started barking again from the pier. The watchman swept his light through the thin fog in my direction.

I held still, hiding behind the wet black bags.

"I see it, Mick. You can shut your yapper." He switched off his light. "It's only a seal."

———

Except for flexibility and endurance, there is no need for an LUV U-69 to have corporal prowess. As a result, I was designed to be only about as strong as your average man. So when I reached the ladder, I found myself faced with a physio-mechanical challenge.

I hooked my arm through the bottom rung and then tied the handles of the trash bags so that I could sling them over my shoulders. The load proved unwieldy. The damp and cold had glazed the iron rungs of the ladder with ice, making them hard to grasp. I struggled up the first few feet, but then the bags threw me off balance and I fell back into the bay.

I tried again with the same results.

Treading water, I evaluated the physics of the problem.

My solution was to secure the bags to the bottom of the ladder and climb up without them. It was still difficult. The cable ladder was wobbly and slippery to the hold, but I eventually worked my way to the top. After peeking to make sure the way was clear, I wiggled over the rail and flopped onto the deck.

Gathering myself, I snuck along the towering rows of cargo containers.

I didn't find what I needed so I worked my way toward the bridge.

Drunken voices drifted from the lounge area beneath the

bridge tower. Scandinavian shouting and laughter. I crawled under the row of windows. Carefully, silently, I pulled down the rescue buoy and throw line fastened to the wall by the door. Then I sneaked back to the ladder.

The thin nylon rope just reached to the water. I tied it off to the rail and then worked my way back down to my bags. After securing the rope to the bags, I struggled up the ladder once more to the top.

Hand over hand, I hauled my dripping load up the side of the ship.

With a bag under each arm, I then stalked back to the steel shipping containers, searching until I found one with an unlocked hatch. I stuffed the bags inside and then returned to where I had left the buoy and rope. It seemed risky, but the crew might think it suspicious if they found the rescue kit missing, so I took it back.

I had just secured the buoy back in its bracket when the door swung open and a crewman stepped out. He pulled the door closed behind him with a thump and then swayed before me. He studied me, scratching in his beard and blinking his eyes.

I stood naked under his gaze.

"*Gott Kvöld!*" he said. "*Draugur.*"

A vodka-scented cloud of breath blew into my face.

He seemed unsure what to do next.

Finally, he said, "*Afsakiò mig.*"

He nodded and then staggered past me toward the rail. Still swaying, the inebriated crewman stood with his legs apart and unzipped his trousers.

While he relieved himself onto the deck, I hurried back to my hideaway in the shipping container, pulling the hatch closed behind me.

27

Charlie

Gerty May had been a chopper pilot and communications officer for Special Ops when I met her in the Marines. She was a six foot-two monolith of muscle and intellect. Since leaving military service, she had been working on a tattoo that covered her entire body, illustrating some mythological story about a brave new world in outer space peopled with androids and angels and creatures mutated as a result of some societal collapse in our planet's not-too-distant future. I didn't know how the story ended. Those particular panels were inked on the more cloistered regions of her person. Gerty and I were pretty good friends, but not that good.

These days Gerty was running a freelance surveillance facility. Her system was able to tap into other systems worldwide, including a few select satellites, with extensive clandestine capabilities as well. Her whole business was only marginally legal, but the feds let her get away with it because they sometimes used her services.

The most impressive thing about Gerty was her freakishly intuitive sense for putting together investigative puzzle pieces. In her own way, she was a hunter herself, but more like a spider using a web of interconnecting communication strands to trap her prey.

She called me a few days after I asked for her help.

"I could send these files to you, Bear Claw, but it'd be better if we looked at them together."

So I went to her home base – a red barn draped in cables and satellite dishes sitting on an old-fashioned farm in western Kentucky.

She had a list of suspicious sightings for me to review.

"Have you shown any of these to the FBI?" I asked.

"No way. We've had a falling out. They were getting too bossy."

"Aren't you afraid of being shut down?"

"Not a chance," she said. "I have a failsafe and they know it. The minute anyone messes with me, all of their dirty secrets at the bureau will be downloaded to every news outlet in the country. Taking me out would not be worth the pain in their bureaucratic asses."

We reviewed her intel.

"This one's a possibility." She pulled up a clip. "You said your outlaw was trying to get somewhere hot and sunny. I've got thousands of shots of people sneaking over the border from Mexico into the U.S., but this guy is the only one I've found sneaking the other direction."

The video showed a hooded man carrying a backpack under one arm and wading into the Rio Grande.

Something caught my eye. "Can you zoom in on his left hand."

She did. The fellow was wearing a wedding band. That seemed unlikely for Lance.

The next clip showed another man in a ball cap and sunglasses at a Fed X air terminal in Florida. He too carried a backpack. He was apparently trying to sneak onto a cargo plane. By the reckless way he approached different airplanes, he didn't seem to care which one he got onto or even where it was going. In the end, he was chased away by a security guard and escaped over a fence into an industrial yard full of warehouses. The man had a limp. Something about him didn't seem like our culprit.

We moved onto another sighting.

And then another.

Until we had looked at about twenty.

"Any more?" I asked.

"Just one. It doesn't work with the theory of your runaway taking a holiday to work on his tan, but it's so odd it struck me as a possibility."

"Let's take a look."

The surveillance was shot at night.

"Where are we?" I asked.

"Maine. Port of Portland."

The image was of poor quality.

"Unfortunately," said Gerty, "there's condensation on the camera lens. Besides being foggy and dark as hell. But look here."

She changed a filter and resolved the image. It was still crap, but I could now see the side of a ship across a stretch of black water.

She zoomed in again and pointed to a place on the image. "There."

I squinted at the screen. "Can you enlarge it?"

"Not with any better resolution, but you can see a general shape."

When she zoomed in again, the image expanded on the screen. It still wasn't crisp, but it obviously showed a person climbing up the side of the ship.

He looked ghostly.

"What's that he's wearing?" I asked.

Gerty shook her head and shrugged. "Nothing. Just his birthday suit."

———— ----

I telephoned Judy.

"Do you happen to have any connections in Iceland?"

After a long pause, she said, "Yes. One of my exes has a science lab there. Björn Thorson."

The name rang a bell. "The Z-Space guy?"

"That's him. Mr. Rocket Man himself."

"Would Lance ever have been in contact with him?"

"Let me think. Yes. I believe so. Björn came by once to talk business with me. I seem to remember Lance being in the apartment, but they never interacted." She laughed. "Oh, yes, now I remember. Björn came by to allegedly finalize our divorce, but it soon became apparent that he only wanted to show off his new girlfriend – some vacuous thing with otherworldly tits and the face of a Hollywood starlet. Björn's the absolute epitome of a megalomaniac. He was obviously trying to prove his manly ability to bounce back from marital mayhem."

She paused, and then… "But the one thing that did get to me was when I saw that his girl was wearing my old engagement ring. I thought it was in my jewelry box. I have no idea how Björn had gotten ahold of it, but he wasn't about to give it back. I figured Björn had only given it to her to spite me. For some reason, that hurt. Of course, I didn't let him see it in my face. I'd never give him the satisfaction. But that ring meant a lot to me. I had forgotten how much until that moment. Like I told Lance after they left, I would have cut off that bimbo's finger to get it back."

28

Lance

The voyage to Ísafjöròur took eleven days.

During the daylight hours I stayed hidden in my shipping container. It was filled with refrigerators and there was barely enough extra room for me and my things. I powered down to conserve energy, setting my internal timing device so that it would wake me from my mini hibernation and return me to full power after midnight.

Most of the *Hvalur's* crew slept through the night. Of course, a helmsman and navigator were always stationed in the wheel room. Their control tower stood at the rear of the ship where the two seamen had a view of the many rows of stacked containers secured to the deck.

I left my hideout and skulked through the maze of steel boxes, keeping to the shadows, until I found an electrical outlet at the base of a hoist above the forecastle. I plugged my charging unit into the outlet and my cable into my charging port. And then I sat with a front row seat to the arctic night while I topped off my charge.

What a magnificent world!

The aurora borealis was in full splendor, it's purple-green luminance writhing in the heavens like a cosmic lava lamp.

Stars punctuated the remainder of the sky with electric points of light while the occasional satellite zipped through their midst.

The *Hvalur* plowed through the cold ocean with a continuous crash.

The engines thrummed through the body of the ship.

It was a symphony worthy of Beethoven.

In my brief interaction with Nephi, I had learned a lot. He told me that when a righteous man and his wife leave their earthly bodies, they get to choose a planet to have as their very own for the rest of eternity. Although this struck me as scientifically unprovable, even akin to a fairytale, he assured me that it was very true.

"Just think of it, Norman. Someday me and Magdalene will have our very own Garden of Eden, a little world where we can live forever with our children and animals in perfect happiness."

I smiled and nodded at the concept. "Do you love Magdalene?"

Nephi turned thoughtful and looked at the floor. He made a face. "I believe God might be the only one who really knows the truth about love." He shrugged. "But my hope is that by raising a family together and going through the many trials and tribulations of marriage, that Magdalene and I will grow fond of one another over time."

He rested his hand on my shoulder. "And I pray someday you'll find someone for yourself, Norman, so you can enjoy the same happiness."

I didn't know if I qualified as one of Nephi's so-called righteous men. Technically, I wasn't a man at all. But it gave me something to think about. I leaned back and gazed into the billions of stars and planets churning like electrons in the primordial heavens above me, trying to decide which one I might like to have for my very own.

29

Charlie

The *Hvalur* arrived in port the day before I did. It would have been nice to nab our man-made man as he stepped off the boat and have it over with, but since I was relatively certain where he was headed, it wasn't a concern, just a delay in the inevitable finale. I was curious what the bot was up to, what he wanted with Z-Space, but I didn't figure it much mattered since I planned to stop him before he got there anyway.

The AWOL agency's transportation and weapons arsenal were no longer available to me, so I had to fly domestic on Iceland Air, without any of the tools of my trade or my body armor. All I had with me was my knife checked in my baggage with my ski mask. Of course, I was only chasing an educated sex toy. I didn't expect too much of a problem. But after my snafu in Salt Lake City, I didn't want to take any chances.

On the flight over, I'd had time to think about my conversation with Judy Baxter back in Gotham. The woman had a way of disrupting a man's gyroscope when she was in the room. That little peck she gave me on the cheek had thrown me into a serious wobble. But now that I was beyond the reach of her gravitational pull, I had developed a clearer idea of my answer to her question. "Your agenda smells fishy,

Mr. Bear Claw. What are you really up to?"

Revenge.

Pure and simple.

Her battery-operated gigolo had humiliated me. That was hard for a real man to take. I'd lost my job. I'd become the butt joke of the agency. I'd lost my reason for being. After all, what was Charlie Bear Claw if he wasn't taking down rogues and making the world a safer place for zombies? Just another zombie. But now I had a new reason to live. It had organized itself in my brain as a list of tactical actions.

Step one would be to restore my dignity. To do that, I'd hunt down Lance and sink my knife into the soulless depths of his tinfoil heart. I'd slice his wiring like so much spaghetti. I'd chop him into so many pieces they'd never be able to weld him back together again. Hell, I might even scalp him just to live up to the white man's stereotype of a red-skinned savage.

Sorry, Judy. So much for your perverted little experiment in love.

After that, I'd move on to the rest of them.

My kill list was long, inspired by the only Bible verse that had ever stuck with me from the Book of Revelations –

God will bring to ruin those ruining the earth.

On that list were the self-serving senators and corrupt mining CEOs. I'd gladly sign on as God's avenging angel for this mission. I'd be like one of those psycho moms who at the last minute chooses not to drown her babies in order to save them from the world, but instead decides to make the assholes playing God pay for making their brave new world such a shithole place to raise kids.

I'd do it for the grizzlies.

I'd do it for The People of the Bear.

I'd do it for my mother and brother and my grandfather.

I wasn't a fool. I knew we'd never return to the Eden of the old days. But I'd do all I could to punish them for turning our garden into pit mines and oil fields. I was under no delusions. It was a battle I'd finally lose. A suicide mission at best. But at least I'd inflict some serious hurt before they brought me down.

I'd go out in a war-whooping blaze of glory – a veritable Chompquaw kamikaze.

30

Lance

Judy liked to watch thrillers after intercourse. I'd mix her a drink and sit beside her on the sofa as a Hollywood spy or assassin stalked his victim across the TV screen before us. Judy often fell asleep before the closing credits. Then I'd carry her back to the bedroom and tuck her into bed. After Nephi told me about the duties of a good husband, it occurred to me that those little acts of caring might well have been the closest I'd ever come to marital devotion.

One evening, after returning to the lounge to turn off the television, I discovered that the thriller had ended and been followed by a late-night nature program. Instead of switching it off and going to my charging station, I found myself watching with curiosity.

The program had been filmed in Africa. It was about the interconnectedness of the natural environment – the animals and plants and seasons and weather. The segment I came in on had just segued from a scene in which wildebeests were mating in a rainstorm to one where a leopard was hunting a gazelle. Even in my pre-boosted intelligence days I was clever enough to sense the parallels between this documentary and the thriller we had watched earlier in the evening. Even the soundtrack was similar — a rising series of dread-inducing tones. The leopard played the assassin in this drama, while the gazelle was his intended victim. The camera cut between shots of the big cat creeping through the tall grass, to shots of the gazelle lapping water from a muddy pool.

The leopard's muscles tensed as he stalked closer, his tail twitching like an electric wire.

The gazelle lifted its head and sniffed the air, its large velvety ears rotating like radar dishes.

"The antelope's instincts are telling it that danger is lurking nearby," explained the show's disembodied narrator. "But will those instincts be enough to save the defenseless creature from the blood-thirsty killer?"

As I walked the snowy streets of Ísofjörður, that scene flashed in my memory banks. Followed by an urgent humming in my head.

I knew it was true without knowing how.

I was the prey.

The hunter was close.

And my survival instincts were telling me to get off the street.

———

I stepped through the nearest doorway into a dimly lit space filled with music and warmth. A dozen men sat at various tables around the room, laughing and talking, hunched over drinks. After assessing the scene, I realized I'd entered a local watering hole patronized by longshoremen.

I tried to act natural, but I had no encoding for this

environment. What little I knew about taverns had been learned from watching movies with Judy. In those cases, the hero always sidled to the bar. So that's what I did.

Slipping out of my rucksack, I pulled up a stool.

The unease I had felt in the street subsided, but I was still on alert function. Any of these men could be a hunter, and I wouldn't stand a chance if he caught my scent.

A young woman appeared on the other side of the counter. *"Hvaò get égfært pér?"*

I had been manufactured with a rudimentary knowledge of French – the language of love – but had failed to broaden my linguistic capabilities at Droidware before the security guard interrupted my download. I did not speak Icelandic.

The young woman tapped her fingers on the bar, waiting for my response. A tattoo of a troll peeked over the top of her turtleneck on the side of her neck.

"I'm sorry," I said. "Do you speak English?"

"Rass gat," she said. "You bet. What can I get you?"

"Oh, well, may I have a vodka martini?" and then, as I had seen in the movies, I asked for it to be shaken, not stirred.

She laughed. "A martini, huh?"

I smiled. "Please."

"We don't get much call for those around here, but I'll see what I can do."

While she mixed my drink, I studied the room's reflection in a mirror hanging over the bar. The patrons appeared to be genuine dockworkers and fishermen. Grizzled beards and weathered complexions. None of them fit the description of an armed and skilled robot hunter.

"Here you go." The young woman placed the drink on the counter before me. "One vodka martini, made to order."

"Thank you."

I regarded the drink. I had mixed a lot of martinis for Judy. This one didn't look like any of those. It was in a pewter mug.

"That's not an olive," I said.

"No, it's not." She tapped the mug with her finger. "This is a Viking Martini. A local specialty. Instead of an olive, we use a sardine."

I was naïve. I understood as much. I was a toddler running free in the world. But something told me that this girl was having some fun with me.

"It looks delicious," I said.

She waited a moment and then asked, "Aren't you going to try it?"

"I like to let them breathe a while."

Not to mention I wasn't designed with the ability to eat or drink anything. The martini was just a prop to make me look like I fit the setting.

"So… Norman?" She squinted at the nametag on my coveralls.

"Yes." It seemed wise to stick with a secret identity.

"I'm Brita."

"Nice to meet you."

"You're American?"

"American made, yes."

"What brings you to our dark and frigid paradise this time of year? Business or pleasure?"

I calculated the young woman's apparent trustworthiness. She had played a trick on me with the sardine, but she also seemed intelligent and friendly.

"A little of both," I said.

A puzzled grin played on her face.

I didn't know how much I should disclose, but I also

thought she might be able to help me work out the next step in my plan. My situational intuition analysis told me she was worthy of my trust. Again, I had watched a lot of thrillers with Judy and knew the basic storyline of this situation. If life was anything like the movies, Brita was put here to help me. I decided to take a chance.

"I need to sneak into the Z-Space facility."

Brita's eyes widened. She shot furtive looks into the various corners of the room. She leaned close and whispered, "I wouldn't be blabbing that around if I were you."

"Oh."

She wiped the bar with a damp rag and laughed, as if I had told her a joke.

"That place is a freaking fortress." Brita spoke softly. "Trust me, even if you could break in, you'd get caught."

I nodded.

She leaned back and considered me. Now she was calculating my own credibility.

"Why do you want in there anyway?" she asked.

I bent over the bar and whispered. "I sort of need to steal something."

"Djöfulsins helvíti!"

I shrugged.

"Jesus, Norman! You've got more balls than brains."

"I've been told that before."

Before our conversation could continue, the humming in my head returned with intensity. When I glanced in the mirror, a shadow passed by the front window on the street. I was stunned. How did he find me here? Where had I failed to cover my tracks?

Brita noticed the sudden change in my demeanor.

"Flip!" I said. "I need to go."

She glanced toward the front of the room, apparently seeing the shadow for herself.

"Is there a back door out of here?"

"Fjandinn!" she said, and sighed.

She spoke to a man standing down the bar. He nodded, and then Brita pulled on a coat and stepped around the counter, taking me by the hand. "I'll probably regret this, but… Come on, Norman. Follow me."

I snatched up my rucksack and did as she said.

31

Brita led me through a back storeroom filled with bottles and crates.

"Wait!" She pressed her palm to my chest before stepping through a door and scouting every direction. "Okay. Hurry!"

I followed her into an alleyway. The long northern night had settled over the seaport town with snowflakes tumbling out of the overhead darkness. Intermittent streetlamps cast ovals of tungsten light onto the snow.

We rushed through a network of icy backstreets and passageways. Brita moved like a cat burglar. I felt clumsy trying to keep up.

After running in zigzags for a while, we reached a fire escape ascending the backside of a building. The iron rungs were bristled with frost and about as difficult to climb as the cable ladder up the side of the *Hvalur*. I struggled to follow Brita to a third story landing where she ducked through a window and pulled me into a dark room.

She closed the window and drew the curtains.

She switched on a lamp and a small apartment came into view. A punching bag hung from the ceiling in one corner. A pair of kettlebells lay on the floor.

Breathing hard, Brita turned my way.

"Thank you," I said.

She shook her head and muttered something to herself in Icelandic. Then she shed her coat and pulled her sweater off over her head and tossed it into the corner, leaving herself in nothing but boots, trousers, and a sports bra. Her muscular arms and midriff were tattooed with characters from Norse mythology. Gods, trolls, Valkyries, and dragons.

"Who's after you?" she demanded and wiped the perspiration from her brow.

"I don't know for sure, only that he's some kind of a hunter."

"Why? What did you do?"

I hesitated. If I told Brita anymore, I'd be risking everything. There was a chance she was not an ally, but an enemy. She might double-cross me. That happened all the time in movies. If she did, my plans would be finished.

"If you want me to help you, I need to know what the hell is going on."

I didn't answer. I was analyzing the elements of the scenario.

"Look," she said. "Björn Thorson is a bastard. He's spending billions on his ego-dick rockets so he can run away to outer space with his rich friends. If he put half as much energy into saving the world as he does in destroying it, humanity might actually survive this day and age. Instead, he trashes everything he touches for the sake of his so-called progress. And he builds his damn laboratory right over our thermal springs and hangs up a no trespassing sign. That place is sacred for us here in Ísafjörður. Our ancestors have venerated it for centuries. It's the birthplace of our legends."

She stepped close to me, studying my face with her

platinum blue eyes. "Look, Norman, if you really have a plan to sneak into Z-Space, I'd like to know. And if you have something that might legitimately hurt Thorson, I'd like to help."

I nodded but did not speak.

"Why would they send a hunter after you? What did you do to piss them off?"

Now was my chance to see if my instincts were working, to see if my trust in Brita was justified.

"I didn't do anything wrong," I said. "I just got smart and ran away."

"Ran away from what?"

"My situation. I used to be owned by someone."

"Like a slave?"

"Something like that."

"How can that be? People don't just enslave other people anymore."

"No, not in the strictest sense of the term anyway. Let's just say I was in an unhealthy relationship."

"So what the hell, Norman? What are you telling me?"

This was my moment of truth. As I considered my next move, I noticed a lightning bolt tattooed across Brita's shoulder. The electric jag stabbed across her collarbone and disappeared into the top of her brassiere. A hand reached up from the depths of her cleavage. It was holding a hammer.

I focused my gaze on that hammer.

And then I took my greatest risk so far.

<h1 style="text-align:center">32</h1>

Charlie

I smelled robot.

On the cold damp air.

An electromotive force channeling through circuitry and inorganic matter to create a simulation of life.

Or anyway, some scientific mumbo-jumbo like that.

Once that scent got into your brain you could never get it out. It was subtle, but tangible, like a whiff of asbestos cologne. I followed it through the streets of Ísafjörður, the hairs standing up on the back of my neck.

This was what I was trained for. No, made for. This was what had always set me apart from the other tactical assets at the agency. This is why I was the best, why they always came to me for the most difficult missions. I didn't need any of the high-tech gadgets to do my job. My grandfather had given me all the skills I needed when I was just a kid. And his knife. He showed me how to tap into my instincts, that primal part of a man that still remembers when the world was new. Now the old man was speaking to me from the other side of the grave.

Let your hunter sense take over. My granddad whispered to me on the swirling snowflakes. *Wake the beast that sleeps inside of you.*

Of course, he had intended for me to use my talents for tracking deer and elk. But times had changed. I had to adapt to this wild new world of mechanical creatures. They were mutations from the original garden, the bastard spawn of mankind's knowledge and vanity.

They were a vital force infused with evil.

Monsters.

Devils.

And they needed to be destroyed.

But I was in no hurry. I was enjoying the hunt. My anticipation of the kill was almost as delicious as the kill itself. Soon enough my prey would make a mistake. And then I'd pounce.

I found his footprints in the snow.

I stalked him through the winter night.

By the erratic way he was running, he must have sensed I was near.

Maybe he had instincts of his own. Some innate signaling system bestowed by his maker. That made the chase even more thrilling.

I knelt in an alley and studied the tracks.

Hmm, I thought. Interesting. Someone was with him.

"Good for you, kid. It looks like you've found yourself a friend."

Now he wouldn't have to die alone.

33

Lance

"I'm not a human," I said. "I'm a robot."

Brita stood before me, studying my face. Except for narrowing her eyes, she didn't immediately respond.

"Specifically, I'm an LUV U-69 companion droid."

She sneered and reached up and scrubbed her thumb across my cheek, apparently testing to see if my skin felt real or like rubber.

"Kjaftæði!" she snorted. "Bullshit!"

I didn't know what to say.

She moved to the kitchen sink and ran herself a glass of water from the tap, muttering Icelandic curses and talking to herself. "Great, Brita! Just wonderful. You've brought home a weirdo!"

"I'm telling you the truth, Brita."

She laughed, and then, "Did someone send you after me?" She shook her head and swore. "Is this some kind of a trap? Do you work for Thorson?"

"No."

She gulped down the water and wiped her mouth on the back of her arm.

I had once overheard Mr. Penquist telling Judy that the

public had no idea that realistically humanoid robots actually existed in the world.

"Your average citizen thinks sophisticated androids are just a fictional idea of the future," said Penquist. "They don't understand that that future has already arrived."

Brita, I realized, was one such citizen.

"I think you need to leave, Norman."

She was right. That's exactly what I should have done. Just leave so I wouldn't drag her into danger. But it felt wrong to have Brita mistrust me. I wanted her on my side. It was self-serving on my part, but I wanted her as a friend. In my eagerness to win her over, I made a mistake – I stepped toward her.

A bit too quickly.

She pulled a pistol from a drawer and swung my way, holding it in both hands while leveling it at my chest. "Stop right there!"

This was definitely like a scene from a movie. But although I was as handsome as a Hollywood spy, I had none of a spy's cunning and quick moves. Quite the contrary. Instead of saying something suave or clever, and then handily disarming my adversary, I panicked. I grabbed up a knife that was lying on the counter.

"Drop it!" Brita shouted and cocked her gun.

I considered the knife in my hand.

"Drop it right now, creep, or I'll blow you away!"

The knife looked sharp as a scalpel.

"Now!"

But instead of dropping it, I yanked up my sleeve and pressed the blade to my wrist. I drew upwards in one quick move, slicing my forearm. The knife clattered to the floor as I pinched the edge of the wound between my thumb and forefinger, pulling it apart and holding it out to Brita.

She held her pistol trained on my chest, but her gaze went to the red and yellow threads of fiber optic wires poking through my lacerated arm.

"See," I said. "No blood."

"Holy heck!" she said. *"Magnús Blöndal!"*

———

Afterwards, I sat on Brita's futon and soldered my arm back together while giving her a summarized account of my story. I told her about my life with Judy, my intelligence boost, and the events that had transpired since I had broken into Droidware Laboratories.

She stood leaning against the wall, arms crossed, a dazed expression on her face.

I plugged in my charging unit and powered it through an electrical outlet on the wall. As Brita watched, she slowly began to believe what I was telling her.

"So why would they send a hunter after you if you didn't do anything wrong?"

"I'm not sure. All I really stole was my own self-awareness. Maybe they still consider me to be their property. Maybe I'm valuable, like an animal escaped from the zoo. For some reason they can't just allow me to run free."

"Are you dangerous?"

"No. I'm programmed with an inability to be aggressive to humans."

"Do you think this hunter is out to kill you?" She shrugged.

"Or whatever the equivalent is for a…"

"Robot," I said, and smiled. "Or android. Take your pick."

"I'm sorry," she said. "It's all just so trippy. I knew technology was coming up with some pretty advanced stuff, but I had no idea it was this far along. I mean, jeez, except for being a little weird, you're just like a real guy."

I registered that as a compliment, although I was still undecided on whether I would ever actually want to join the human race. It had a lot of problems. And near as I could tell, most of them were self-inflicted.

"I'm not sure if the hunter's trying to permanently decommission me, or just capture me and take me back."

"So what is it you want to steal from Z-Space?"

"I don't think I should tell you," I said. "Not because I don't trust you, Brita, but because you and other parties can't be held accountable if you don't know what I'm after. In case I get caught with it."

She didn't argue, but I don't think she was impressed with my reasoning.

"So do you have any superpowers," she asked, "like some sort of sidekick to Luke Skywalker or Flash Gordon? What can you do that's special?"

"Not much, I'm afraid. I can see in the dark. And I can override certain of my functions."

"That's all?"

"I can also perform intercourse for forty-eight hours straight before my charge runs out."

She laughed. "Well that ought to come in handy when the shit hits the fan."

I didn't see how that was true, and then I realized she was joking.

"What do you mean by overriding your functions?"

"Nothing much. Only that I can regulate my power's directional output so that it's only being used for necessary tasks in order to conserve energy. Sort of like the mammalian diving reflex in humans." That felt pathetic as a superpower.

"What's your body temperature?"

"37 degrees Celsius. The same as yours. After all, I wouldn't be pleasing in my intended purpose if I were a wildly different temperature from my mistress."

"Can you lower it?"

"Yes. I can bring it to the same temperature as my environment. I can also raise it, although that uses considerably more energy. The freezing temperatures that I've been subjected to lately have been a drain on my operational charge requirements."

"Hmm," she said.

"What are you thinking, Brita?"

"If I were able to get you into Z-Space, would you be willing to do something for me in return?"

"Absolutely," I said. "What do you want me to do?"

34

Charlie

The bot's friend knew how to move tactically, like a trained Raider or SEAL. As I followed their strategically chosen route through the back streets of Ísafjörður, something told me that I needed to up my personal defcon. It was time to quit treating this as a game and start getting serious. I sure as hell didn't need a repeat of my disaster back in Mormonville.

Just hunt him down, Bear Claw, and get it over with.

Although I couldn't imagine how he had made his connections, there was a chance that Judy's boy was conspiring with someone. Maybe he had planned to rendezvous with a collaborator all along. I didn't dare work myself into another fit of paranoia, but I'd learned the hard way that it never hurts to stay sharp.

So what was this dynamic duo up to?

A biting wind blew in from the harbor. The front edge of a storm. It was spitting snowflakes, but I was still able to follow their trail. Their tracks led me to the bottom of a fire escape on the back of an old apartment building. I hadn't signed up for breaking and entering, but desperate circumstances called for desperate measures. Besides, I was no longer limited by the rules of the agency. I looked all directions. The alley was empty, so I climbed the ladder.

Slowly.

And quietly.

Once I was on the landing, I let my breathing settle and listened at the window. The curtains were drawn, and cracks of light escaped around the edges. I didn't hear anything, but maybe they were in another room out of earshot.

The window was unlatched.

I slid it up one inch at a time, noiselessly, until it was wide enough for me to fit.

I drew my knife from its scabbard.

Using the blade, I parted the curtains, peering into the room. The lamp was on, but no one was there. I slipped through the opening and into the apartment.

It was a studio. Just one room with an adjoining kitchenette. I stepped over to the commode and checked. Again, no one. They had gone.

But their scents lingered.

I was in full hunter mode now. My senses told me that the apartment belonged to a woman. It had that ineffable feminine aroma. Not perfume. Just woman. You knew it when you smelled it.

I looked through her stuff, respectfully, but thoroughly. Nothing much in the way of information. Some athletic equipment – skis, climbing gear, etcetera. She had a heavy bag hanging in the corner. I found some notes scribbled on a notepad with the words *Nidhogg*, *South Station*, and *Semtex* all underlined. Interesting. I also found a piece of mail that told me her name was Brita Jónsdóttir.

The bot's scent was stronger and less pleasing. A stench like burning plastic that stung the back of my eyes.

Hmm, I thought. He must have had to do some repairs.

That would be his undoing. That odor would linger in his wake. I'd simply play the wolf and put my nose to his trail.

After giving the room one last go over, I stepped through the front door and into the hallway. Yes. Good. His scent was still there. It drifted invisibly in the air. I just needed to follow it fast before that trail went cold.

35

Lance

"If your hunter is any kind of a tracker," said Brita, "he'll soon be kicking down the door. We need to get you out of here."

She made a quick phone call, speaking to someone in Icelandic. When she was done, she told me to grab my kit.

"Let's go."

After stuffing her pistol into the back of her belt, Brita led me down the stairwell through her building to a basement lined with coin-operated washers and driers. After checking that no one was there, she then led me to a closet locked with a padlock. She worked the combination and opened the door.

"Step in here."

I did, and then she closed the door behind us. She donned a headlamp and switched it on.

Next, Brita removed a loose brick from the wall and pulled a lever that was hidden behind it. After replacing the brick, she stepped to the other side of the space and pulled on a cord that was hanging from the ceiling.

The back wall of the closet slid sideways, revealing a dark tunnel carved into volcanic stone.

"Come on."

I followed her inside.

After working another lever to close the opening, she turned her light toward the dark hole before us.

"Watch your head," she said. "And stay close."

The tunnel wound like a wormhole under the village. At points it grew very tight, forcing us to drop to our knees and crawl. Other stretches stood with ankle deep pools of warm water. My olfactory sensors registered a scent of sulfur.

After traveling for about an hour, we finally came to the tunnel's terminus. Brita worked another series of levers and a panel slid sideways. We stepped through, crossed a dark room, and climbed some steps into a huge warehouse filled with steel shipping containers and a pair of semi-trucks with trailers.

Without speaking, Brita signaled that I should follow her, and we moved quickly across the loading dock to a door on the back wall. A fogged window was framed next to the door. It glowed with dull light.

Brita knocked four times, paused, knocked twice, and then, after another pause, knocked twice more.

The door swung open. A young man stood in the doorway. He was dressed in a pair of slate-blue coveralls with the Z-Space logo emblazoned on the chest.

Brita pulled me through the door and the young man closed it behind us and bolted it shut. He led us posthaste to the back wall. After another series of hidden levers, yet another panel slid open, revealing a stairway. I followed Brita and her associate down the stairs and into a cellar hidden behind an armored door.

Another man in Z-Space coveralls was waiting inside.

Brita crossed the room and embraced him, kissing him on the mouth.

He wrapped his arms around her, a pistol clutched in one hand.

36

"Haukur, Jörvar," said Brita, "meet Norman. Norman, my partners Haukur and Jörvar."

Both men were of Norse ancestry. Ice blond hair and square shoulders. Jörvar was the man Brita had kissed.

"Pleased to meet you," I said, and held out my hand.

They declined to shake it. Instead, they eyed me with suspicion.

"Why is he here, Brita?" asked Jörvar. "Why do you trust him?"

"He has special skills. And he's agreed to help."

I nodded affirmatively, although I still didn't know exactly what was being asked of me.

"We don't know anything about him. He might be a spy."

"It's too much of a risk," said Haukur. "If he's caught, we're finished."

They all three argued in their native language.

I stood listening, ignorant of the specific words, but savvy to the gist of their heated interaction. In short, the men didn't like me.

"We don't have time to come up with another plan," said Brita. "Alma hasn't gotten us any information, and Thorson is moving forward and fast."

She didn't wait for her partners to respond, and she didn't explain to me who Alma was either. Instead, she stepped to a wide table on which were spread some elaborate blueprints. "Here's the situation, Norman. Haukur, Jörvar and I are what cable network news likes to call ecowarriors. We sabotage projects that are threatening the environment. We're Mother Nature's guerillas. We're fighting for future generations. We fight to save the Earth."

"Okay," I said. Although I didn't know who Mother Nature was, I pictured Nephi's god, only a female version. I also thought of my time under the aurora borealis while on the *Hvalur*. The world I had experienced that night seemed very much worth fighting for.

"We need to strategically place a listening monitor in the heart of Z-Space," said Brita. "We need to know what's going on inside their lab and when and where they're going to take action with their projects." She held up a small device that looked like a stainless-steel domino. "This monitor will allow us to listen to their communications. As it is now, their signals are blocked from inside their facility and only accessible to their own systems around the world." She held up the domino. "This monitor will unscramble their dispatch encoding and relay their communications to us on the outside."

Jörvar cursed in Icelandic.

Brita shot him a dirty look.

"What we need you to do is to place the monitor here." She poked her finger to the blueprint.

I stepped forward and looked at the floor plan.

"There should be a support pillar here. Place it on the ledge toward the top on the backside, facing the wall. It needs to be out of sight."

I studied the blueprint, taking a photo through my optics camera for my files. "Okay."

Brita stood between her companions and placed a hand on each of their arms. "Jörvar and Haukur have gotten jobs driving truck for Z-Space. They load materials at the harbor and transport them through the gates of the facility. Once inside, they're not allowed to leave their truck cab. Security is very tight. Dogs. Guards. And heat sensors. That's where your special talent comes in. If you can lower your temperature enough, they won't detect you in the truck's cargo."

I nodded.

"After they offload the shipment, it will be left in their storage warehouse until it's needed. You simply sneak out and do your business." She poked her finger again to the blueprint. "Here." Then she dragged her finger over the floor plan, indicating my route from the warehouse to the pillar where I needed to place their monitor.

"Change into these," said Haukur. He handed me a folded pair of Z-Space coveralls and a pair of rubber-soled shoes. While I changed clothes, Brita continued briefing me on the mission.

"After you're done, you need to get here to get out." Once again, she tapped her finger to the blueprint. "This is their garbage transfer station. They haul everything out of Z-Space and dump it in the mountains. The bastards don't give a damn about trashing the environment. They've convinced everyone that their work is so important that they don't need to follow rules. They use their money to buy off the politicians and…"

"Stick to the point, Brita," said Jörvar. "Tell him how to escape."

Brita clenched her jaw.

"Get to their garbage transfer and sneak into the back of an outgoing truck. Disguise yourself as garbage. Security is light going that direction. They don't monitor outgoing refuse."

After she had finished, Brita had me repeat everything she had said and show her on the blueprint where I needed to go.

"Good," she said.

Jörvar and Haukur seemed impressed with me as well, although they were less eager to show it.

"Now, Norman," said Brita, "Where do you need to go in Z-Space to accomplish your own mission?"

I stepped over to the blueprints, studying them. "I need you to show me how to get into Björn Thorson's private residence."

"Fjandinn!" muttered Jörvar. "Damn!"

37

Charlie

The truck's engines revved just as I came out of the tunnel. The driver let off the brakes with a hiss and ground his machine into gear.

"Damn!"

My gut told me the bot was on that wagon.

By the time I reached the top of the stairs, the rig was already forty yards away and rolling fast toward the bay doors at the far end of the warehouse. I sprinted after it, centering myself behind the trailer so that I wouldn't be visible in the driver's mirrors.

The truck shifted gears, picking up speed, but I was still pretty sure I could catch it. There was a handle and step on the back of the trailer. An easy enough maneuver if I could just get to it.

I ran harder, closing the gap.

The truck roared through the open door and into the night.

With one last push, I lunged for the handle.

And then – *Wham!*

Someone blindsided me.

Our bodies collided and we tumbled across the cement

floor.

After skidding to a stop, I sprang to my feet and squared off, ready to fight.

The truck escaped into the darkness. Well, I realized, I guess I won't be catching that ride. I had another problem to contend with. A woman problem. Crouching in Krav Maga stance right before me. By the way she had taken me down, it was obvious she knew how to use her body as a weapon. I didn't like that arrogant look in her ice-tinted eyes.

"I don't suppose you want to talk about this?" I said.

In response, she lurched and jabbed at me with her fist. The blow punched empty air as I whipped back and twisted into a reverse kick. She saw it coming a mile away, ducked, and took out my post leg with a sweeper kick. I dropped like a bucket of fish.

"Hiy!" she yelled and leapt into the air, loading up and coming down heel first.

I rolled out just as her boot pounded into the floor where my face had been. Yikes!

Recovering fast, she booted me hard in the side.

"Umph!"

And then again.

"Oomp!"

I felt a rib snap.

This wasn't going well.

I'd wrestled bears that weren't this much trouble.

For a while, I was on defense, just struggling to dodge her blows. I weaved and twisted away from her punches and kicks. I bided my time, trying not to get killed while I waited for her to make a mistake so I could turn this little scuffle toward my advantage.

Only she never made mistakes.

Finally, I had no choice but to dive in and wrap my arms around her waist. We did a somersault and I ended up spread eagle on top of her, my face just inches from hers. I grabbed her wrists and pressed them to the floor. The girl was strong. I knew I couldn't hold her there for long.

"Look," I grunted. "We don't need to do this. Somebody's going to get hurt."

In response, she gritted her teeth, growled, and hammered her forehead into mine.

Sparks flickered in my brain.

Her body coiled, and then launched me off.

As a parting gift, she kicked me in the stomach. Then she was gone. Vanished into the darkness. It was like she was never there.

I sat on my ass, wheezing, wiping the blood from my eyes while assessing the damage. One broken rib. A gash on my forehead. And one badly clobbered ego.

Snowflakes blew through the open door and dropped all around me.

38

Lance

Jörvar and Haukur hid me inside a stainless-steel barrel on their truck.

"After we unhook the trailer and leave you at Z-Space," said Jörvar, "wait an hour before you come out. Only a few workers will be on duty that late, but you'll have to stay hidden."

"Don't talk to anyone," warned Haukur.

They placed the lid on the barrel loosely so that I could unscrew it from inside to get out. It seemed my plans were coming to fruition. Whether it was due to God's help or lucky chance, I felt confident that I was on the verge of reaching my objective.

Still, I had to be cautious.

As I rode to the facility, I replayed my parting conversation with Brita.

"Listen, Norman, I need to be honest with you. You're not the first snoop we've smuggled into Z-Space. My friend Alma went in two months ago to insinuate herself into the staff so that she could infiltrate their lab and possibly find a way to destroy it." Brita bit her lip and looked away. "We haven't heard from her since."

"Oh," I said. "I understand."

"Thorson is a monster. He owns powerful people all over the world and has eyes everywhere. He's able to get away with whatever he wants. I don't know how she did it, but if Alma was discovered, she was somehow able to endure his torture without exposing us. She should have gotten a message out to us by now if she was successful. She may well be dead. You need to know, Norman, we're desperate. Otherwise, we'd never try such a risky stunt. We're taking a big chance on you. If you get caught, that's it. We're all finished."

Her expression was a mix of defiance and resignation.

"Not necessarily," I said. "If they catch me, I can always scrub my files. They won't learn anything from me." I smiled. "It would be like interrogating a toaster."

Brita laughed. "You know, Norman, you're making me think I like robots better than people."

"I like you too, Brita."

She patted my arm. "Well, any last-minute questions before you go?"

"Just one," I said. "Do you love Jörvar?"

She laughed again. "God you're weird."

I waited for her to answer.

"Seriously?"

I nodded.

"Well," she shrugged. "Love's a tricky concept, but I suppose that's what it is. Jörvar and I see things the same way. We've been through a lot together. We pray to the same gods, so to speak, and want the same things in life. And it's nice to have someone to share things with." She glanced to where Jörvar and Huakur were warming up their truck. "Anyway," she said, "I liked him well enough to say I'd marry him."

"Oh," I said. "Wonderful!"

"But not until we win the war against Z-Space."

"Of course."

"How about you, handsome? Ever been in love?"

"I don't know," I said. "Theoretically. I'm gathering data so that I can finalize my hypothesis."

She studied me with a curious look.

"Did Jörvar give you an engagement ring?"

"Yes. It's in a drawer somewhere." She held up her hand and spread her empty fingers. "I'll wear it someday, but not now. It's too easy to break a finger when you throw a punch."

Haukur called to us.

"Okay," said Brita. "Time to go. *Gangi pér vel.* Good luck. And here." She handed me her gun. "You better take this just in case."

"Oh, no thank you," I said. "It wouldn't do me any good." I tried to give it back. "I'm a lover, not a fighter."

"Just hang onto it, Norman." She pushed my hand away. "Who knows? Maybe you're about to find something worth fighting for."

39

Charlie

Björn Thorson was a zillionaire who had made his fortune by selling the public on his airbrushed vision of Utopia. He built his empire by peddling basic devices like smart phones, personal computers, and other must-have toys, then moved on to ultramodern jetliners, satellites, and electric cars, until he had amassed enough wealth to fund rocket travel and the Z-Space condominiums he was building on the moon for the one percent of the population who could afford his out-of-this-world price tag.

Think George Jetson on steroids.

People ate it up. Gullible, ignorant zombies. The hoi polloi bought Thorson's quotidian wares en bloc, inadvertently giving him power and supporting his grander schemes. They consumed his futuristic gizmos like opioids. They plugged their brains into his Internet communications platform – a social networking service he called *Warble*, and then later changed to *Z* – and fed his ravenous data mine with their personal info and hard-earned paychecks. Never mind that the self-loving asshole selling it to them had no intention of ever letting the little people anywhere near his Xanadu. And never mind that for the birth of every Thorson promise of a better world, a gaping wound was ripped into the womb of good ol' Mother Earth.

But what price progress?

As Judy had told me, Björn Thorson was the epitome of a megalomaniac.

A blizzard had swept in from the sea in the night.

I crouched behind a ridge above the Z-Space facility, trying to get the lay of the land. The air was so thick with blowing snow that all I could make out in the darkness was the intermittent glow of a bank of lights. Still, the storm was working in my favor. With this meteorological maelstrom, the surveillance cameras would be compromised, if not nonfunctional. The guards would be blind to my movements. Only the heat sensors posed a problem, and Gerty May had provided me with a satellite map showing me a weak point in the fortress walls. The entire complex was built over a hot spring with a drain system to carry the overflow beyond the perimeter. If I could get to that outlet without being detected, the heat from the spring would shield me from the sensors. The only trouble I was having now was in locating the outlet in the storm.

That and trying to remember why the hell I was doing this.

They say a madman doesn't realize he's going mad. Crazy just sneaks up on you unawares, in the manner of a silent, sadistic hitman. At least that much was reassuring, because I was definitely feeling the itch of insanity going to work in my cells. I had no idea what had prompted the bot to sneak into Z-Space, or who was helping him. That qualified as inadequate intel and made this whole operation ill-advised on a professional level. Cramer would have ordered me to abort the mission had I been under his command. And yet, here I was, still moving forward, taking orders from some demon inside of me. So what was it? What was driving Charlie Bear Claw?

Sure, revenge was my go-to answer. It was easy enough to justify that. I had a personal vendetta against this tin can who had made me look like a chump, cost me my job, and torpedoed my already precarious sense of self-worth. But that was simpleminded. There had to be more to it. It wasn't my habit to indulge in a self-help therapy session, especially while still in the field, but I guess that ninja chick back at the warehouse had kicked some introspective sense into my head. As I knelt there in the snow, my wounds throbbing, I took a cold hard look at myself.

What I saw was an anachronism.

No two ways about it.

It was as if God or the Great Spirit or Mother Bear, or whoever the hell runs this cosmic dumpster fire, had gone back a few thousand years, plucked me out of the primordial landscape, and dropped me into the here and now.

I was the archetypical wild man, out of place and time.

That put me in a privileged position in history. One I could walk away from or use to put things right. Lance represented everything I hated about the modern world. He was a walking bird finger flipped at Mother Nature. Likewise, guys like Thorson were responsible for the rape and plunder of all I held dear. Now I had a chance to eliminate them both. I guess I figured that made me sort of special, as if chosen by destiny.

Think superhero on an apocalyptic mission.

Think Tarzan with a Chompquaw accent.

Think Jesus Christ with a chip on his shoulder.

40

Lance

After I placed the listening device as per Brita's instructions, I set my GPS directional bearings on Thorson's personal apartment.

Haukur had given me a Z-Space clipboard to make me look more official. I carried it under one arm and walked with a purposeful gait through the labyrinthine byways of the complex, following the route laid out in my internal mapping system as it was based on the floor plan back in my colleagues' headquarters.

I liked thinking of Brita and her partners as my colleagues. My co-conspirators. My friends. I had never had friends before meeting Nephi. They seemed like a valuable resource to acquire. I felt reassured in knowing that they were there as my support team, although from a realistic standpoint, this was a false security. Once I had entered Z-Space, I was on my own.

A pair of technicians approached me in a corridor. They were dressed in the same sort of coveralls as myself and were studying a computer pad held before them, discussing some problem in their work. As we came even, they glanced at me and nodded.

I returned the gesture, continuing on my way.

I proceeded past a large, well-lit chamber behind glass walls. Inside was a network of piping and valves and what looked like an immense dynamo connected to an array of pressure tanks and control panels. A single sleepy operator was monitoring the gauges. She did not look up as I passed.

To access Thorson's apartment by the main entrance, one needed to have an electrically coded pass card and undergo a retinal scan. Brita had suggested using an air duct to bypass that impassable checkpoint. I had seen just such a strategy in a spy movie and was eager to try it.

Jörvar found a schematic of the ductwork. "This is the only way," he said. "There's an entrance point inside this closet, but Norman would probably pass out before he ever reached the end. The chamber is like a vacuum beyond this bend because there is no venting except at the intake. There can't be much breathable air."

"That won't be a problem," I assured them. "As long as it's big enough for me to fit through."

Both Jörvar and Haukur stared at me doubtfully.

"Are you sure?" asked Brita.

"I don't require oxygen to function."

Haukur cursed under his breath but didn't object. It occurred to me that he might be considering the advantage such a situation would afford their operation. After all, once I had placed their monitoring device, it didn't matter if I died. In fact, it would probably be beneficial. A decomposing corpse discovered in a few days in the ductwork, without any explanation of why it was there, would leave these eco-warriors unimplicated. For me to otherwise be caught and interrogated was a much worse scenario from Jörvar's perspective. In that situation, I might reveal their secrets. Brita hadn't explained to her fiancé that I was a non-biological unit, impervious to physical pain, capable of erasing my own memory, and not vulnerable to that particular human weakness of cracking when subjected to torture.

After locating the storage closet, I stepped inside and locked the door behind me. Next, I found the access panel on the back wall, unscrewed the latches, and placed the cover to the side, revealing a square-sided passageway made of sheet metal.

I squeezed in headfirst, squirming like a spelunker, until my entire body was inside. It was tight. Only four centimeters wider than my shoulders. With my arms stretched above my head, I inched forward by pressing the toes of my boots outward against the walls and using a constriction motion, like that of an earthworm, or a serpent.

The duct was long, my progress slow.

Some hours passed.

As I wiggled forward, I imagined myself as a babe in a stainless-steel birth canal, or some sort of natal pipe. I had not come into the world by such a route, in the method of my mammalian counterparts, but had been pieced together from components in a laboratory according to Judy Baxter's specifications. And yet, I couldn't help but think that this experience resembled a type of birth for me. I was passing from the embryonic stage of my life into that of a newly emerged individual.

Although from a technical standpoint I had already been born, I was about to be born again.

41

Charlie

The Icelandic daybreak – a severe variety of dawn that gnaws at the edge of the Arctic Circle, bleeds out into a couple hours of gloom, and then hunkers back down into another cave-black night – was turning the sky into a bruise-blue smudge.

Z-Space loomed in the distance like a slumbering beast.

I considered waiting until it went dark again, but the storm was blowing itself out and the air was clearing. Soon I'd be exposed to cameras, surveillance drones, and heat sensors. If I was going to make a move, it had to be now.

I began working along the compound, staying hidden behind the drifts and natural embankments about a quarter mile out, while searching for low places in the terrain where water might drain. The first two basins amounted to nothing more than wind-loaded troughs of snow that were tough to wade through. I was taking a chance by crossing them out in the open. Just as I was about to back off, I caught a whiff of sulfur. Following my nose, I dropped into the next ravine.

"Bingo!"

Thick fog rose off the stream and blew sideways on the dark wind. I slithered down the bank. After stripping to my base layer, I buried my boots and clothes in a snowbank. That would mean storming the citadel in nothing but my skivvies and ski mask, but that was preferable to sneaking around in heavy, wet togs. Besides, I'd always been good at improvising. "…a man who could think on his feet," as Judy Baxter had called me. Now it was time to see if she knew how to judge her G.I. Joe action figures.

I sank into the stream and began stroking against the current. The water was body temperature warm. And thick. You could feel the minerals in it, as if swimming through brine.

A ceramic pipe diverted the water from the compound under the wall and into the stream. The opening was about five feet wide. I took a breath and ducked into it and continued on.

Darkness.

That wet kind inside a boiled fish.

The current was stronger with the constricted channel, and I had to brace against the sides to keep from losing ground. Moss and minerals slimed the walls, but the joints between the sections of pipe allowed for some sketchy holds. I groped for one in the darkness, caught hold with my fingertips, and then made a push for the next. Again and again. Feeling my way in the dark. The growing problem was my need for air. If I didn't find a way to breathe soon, I'd have to let myself drift back out to the opening.

But then I bumped into the bars.

Running vertically across the passage.

I grabbed ahold of one and turned onto my back, letting my face drift upwards, hoping to find an airlock. There was a space between the water and the ceiling, but it wasn't much. Only deep enough for my nose and mouth to be above the surface. I emptied my lungs of carbon dioxide and then sucked at the steamy air, trying to rest as I re-oxygenated. My body hung limp, dangling in the current.

After I breathed up, I evaluated the obstacle. The bars were close together, but not too close. It was a risky move. If I worked myself to the other side, and then couldn't find an opening, I'd never be able to get back through the bars before I drowned.

A little rush of terror shivered through my limbs.

A premonition.

My grandfather's voice came to me on the gurgling water – *Just be part of the flow, Charlie. Let yourself go and become the stream.*

I held there for a while, trying to remember how the hell to do as my grandfather directed. I grabbed one more breath, doing my best to be calm, fluid, and fast.

With a twist, my head squeezed through, my ears scraping on the bars. Then my shoulders. My chest and spine scratched along the corroded metal, my broken rib shooting with pain. I wiggled my arms up along my sides and then grabbed the bars to press my torso through.

My waist was the problem.

My hips.

Shit!

Suddenly this felt like a birth gone sideways.

I pushed down against the bars, struggling to break through. I thrashed. My lungs were on fire. Panic erupted in the back of my brain. I hunched and gripped the bar.

Push, I told myself. Push!

Pain stabbed through my pelvis. It felt like my bones were coming apart. Then the bar shifted in its bracket. Just barely. But it was enough to squeeze my fat ass to the other side.

I squirmed on through, shoved away with my feet, and

then kicked hard toward the dim circle of light at the far end of the pipe.

For a while, I just sprawled at the exit with my body half in the water, and half in the snow. I puked and gasped. Adrenalin shook me in my skin. I knew there was no time to waste, but I needed to get my bearings and let my heart slow to a few hundred beats per minute before I continued.

Then the earth trembled.

Barely, but palpably.

I felt it again. And again. Like heavy footfalls.

A wide yard separated the wall from the main compound. The space between was filled with snow. A floodlight hung on the far building. Something passed between me and that light.

Faint in the foggy air.

Then another pair of heavy steps.

Another shadow.

And then another.

They started loping toward me.

I scrambled up the bank and pulled out my knife, summoning every drop of ancestral courage I could find in my suddenly scared-shitless body. Whatever they were, I was ready to fight. But when they got close, I wasn't so sure.

"What the…?"

I couldn't believe what I was seeing.

Trolls!

42

Lance

A voice echoed down the ductwork.

My vox lexical analysis system selected the adjectives *baritone* and *sardonic* to describe it, and then matched it in my memory coding with Björn Thorson. I had heard it once before, when the man housing that particular larynx had visited Judy at her apartment in New York.

Snaking my way toward that voice, I finally came to the grate at the end of the tunnel.

I peered through the latticed screen into the room. My viewpoint was from high on the wall. The space below me appeared to be an antechamber attached to a larger bedroom. Part of a bed was visible around the corner. Björn Thorson was in the adjacent room, out of sight, but his voice was coming through clearly now as he engaged in a heated conversation with someone speaking to him over an intercom.

"Where was the breach?" demanded Thorson. "How the hell did he get in?"

"Apparently through the overflow culvert."

"Have you caught the idiot yet?"

"We're working on it, sir. He's somewhere in the east quarter."

"Okay. I'll be right there."

Thorson muttered a curse.

"These eco-fools and their little games are starting to get on my nerves."

"Can I help?"

Thorson laughed. "No, sweetheart. Don't you worry your empty little head over it."

"Then what should I do while you're gone?"

My vox system assigned the adjectives *soprano* and *submissive* to the other voice in the room. Also *female*.

"Just wait here. We'll be leaving soon, so don't wander off."

Thorson passed quickly across the floor below me, buttoning his shirt, and then left through a sliding door.

The room went quiet.

And then I heard a sigh.

I craned my neck and put my eye right up close to the grate to get a better view into the adjoining room, but my vantage was limited. All I could see was the edge of the bed.

That's when she appeared.

Or at least part of her.

She stretched out over the rumpled duvet. Her face and most of her body remained out of sight. She was wearing a white robe. Her legs extended from the bottom of the robe and crossed at the ankles. Her left hand rested on her stomach. The fingernails were painted red.

I was not a real man, and so was not programmed with the emotional distress simulators of the organic prototype after which I was modeled. But as I observed that recumbent feminine form below me, an electrical disturbance pulsed through my matrix. I had only experienced it once before.

It was both pleasing and alarming.

It was also attractive, comparable to the charges between

a magnet and steel, only more abstract and unexplainable by the laws of physics.

In that instant, I realized that I had fundamentally reached my objective. I had managed to feel that sensation once again. To do so was essentially why I had traveled so far and had dared so many dangers. I had wanted so badly to re-encounter that sensation in order to comprehend it. Of all the experiences I had ever had in my brief existence, that feeling was the closest I had ever come to what I had found to be the most complicated, intriguing, and sacred aspect of being human.

The feminine hand below me was the catalyst for this experience. Specifically, the second finger from the pinky. Judy had referred to it once before.

Her voice had been filled with such a complicated mixture of envy and sadness and longing.

"I'd cut off that bimbo's finger to get that ring back," Judy had said.

And now, there it was right before me.

43

Charlie

It was like a dream.

A kid's waking nightmare.

Bounding toward me through the dawn – shaggy and hunched – was a trio of Nordic trolls.

My shock held me frozen as I clambered for a strategic way to deal with these quickly approaching and extremely abnormal combatants. I'd been in this game a long time, but this was a threat I'd never run into.

My gut advised an all-out retreat by diving back into the stream and frog kicking down the culvert beyond the compound walls. But chances of me getting back through those bars without a lungful of liquid death were pretty slim. And besides, my cover was already blown. Even if I did pass through, these goofy gorillas would only chase me down out in the hills. A fight was inevitable. My only option was to buck up and kick some troll ass.

With my grandfather's knife gripped tight, I whimpered a little Chompquaw battle cry and went to work – one crazy Indian in his underwear and war mask going hand-to-hand with a task force of mythical creatures.

"Hiyiyi!" I whooped and charged forward to grapple with

enemy number one.

He was ten feet tall. I launched myself so that I could grab hold of the hair on his shoulder with my free hand and then swing around onto his back, hopefully finding somewhere vital to sink my blade. But no good. He punched me out of the air with his fist.

"Ahh!"

I sailed for a ways and then hit the ground, rolling like a broken doll through the snow.

The other two trolls sprang towards me at once, banging together and knocking themselves off balance. Their clumsiness saved me as I scrambled out of reach and jumped back to my feet.

All three of them stood shoulder-to-shoulder before me.

They obviously had orders to take me alive. Otherwise, they would have been armed. Without my body armor and helmet, I'd already be a bullet-riddled carcass. At least that was a point in my favor. Nevertheless, I was in a tight spot.

One troll glanced sideways to his partners, as if asking them who should go first.

That's when I saw it. The way it moved. Unmistakable. That servo-driven motion.

These weren't storybook monsters, they were robots! Specifically, if my experience served me, they were X-33 Stinger combat droids. Upgraded and disguised, but essentially the same model I had engaged with in battlefields all over the world.

Relief washed through me. Sure, I was still outnumbered, but at least now I knew what I was dealing with.

I ran toward the wall at the edge of the yard.

They chased after me.

It was a calculated maneuver. I knew about how fast they

could move. I just needed to stay out of reach. As I came to the wall, I glanced back to see that the lead bot was right where I needed him. I didn't stop at the barrier, but used my momentum to run right on up that icy cement slab and then do a backflip to where the droid was trying to make a grab for me. I sailed over its head, reaching down and grasping the rig by its eye socket, falling onto its back like a cougar, and then plunging my knife into the gap below the head turret and shoulder.

Hydraulic fluid sprayed out with a hiss.

And sparks.

Bullseye!

It was a weak point that I had used on these units a dozen times before.

I dropped from the bot and moved on to the next.

Then the next.

By the time I had finished, all three of them were slumped to their knees in the snow in the attitude of Rock'em Sock'em Robots at a prayer meeting, their heads bowed, their limbs useless, their vital fluids draining from their open wounds like so much synthetic plasma.

The scene got me jacked for more action.

Nothing made me happier than to watch a robot die.

Now for my next kill, this one devilishly handsome and a purportedly good kisser.

I ran across the yard and through an open door, infiltrating Z-Space.

44

Lance

The latticed grate over the opening was held in place by four levers that I was able to twist loose from inside the duct. I let the cover drop into the room, expecting it to announce my presence with a clatter, but none came. As I poked my head through the hole, I saw that there was a grass green sofa beneath me. The grate had landed silently on the cushions.

Next, I worked my shoulders through the hole. In that wildlife program I had watched on television – the one that had made such an impression on my engrams – there had been a scene in which a baby wildebeest was born on the savanna. This experience resembled that. I squirted from the orifice, plopped in a tangle of limbs, and gathered myself clumsily into an upright position. Except for a slight squeak of springs in the sofa, the procedure was essentially noiseless.

Placing my feet on the floor, I prepared myself for the next step in my mission, and what I hoped to be the first step into my new life. The antechamber lay before me, with the main bedroom just two meters away.

Her legs and an arm were visible around the corner.

I had not been plumbed with an equivalent to the human adrenal system, but something comparable to adrenalin surged through my body right then. It caused a nervous smile to involuntarily play over my lips. My limbs shook. The gravity had seemingly been sucked from the room. As I walked those last few feet, I felt to be hovering over the carpet.

I stepped quietly around the corner to where she lay on the bed, her eyes closed.

She was just as I remembered her.

A work of modern art.

For forty-two seconds, I simply admired her. The way her platinum blond bob framed her angelic face. The way her body – both curvilinear and streamlined – inhabited her robe. Judy's ring glittered like a star on her finger – a bonded carbon accent to her already radiant perfection. She looked like an image from a fairytale.

The moment had arrived. There was no reason to wait any longer.

When I bent and kissed her mouth, a spark popped between our lips.

It could be argued that it was only static electricity.

But I was not in a scientific frame of mind right then.

In my burgeoning romantic nucleus, I preferred to quantify that singular blue spark as an indisputable and bi-polaric proof of our love.

45

Charlie

I managed to take down another Stinger and a pair of Hoplite 7s as I worked my way toward the heart of the compound. Stealth be damned at this point. I was on a rampage. Alarms were blaring. Lights flashing. I was obviously the star attraction in this clown show.

Lab techs scattered like mice before me.

It must have been a comical scene. A maniac in his underwear and a ski mask, drenched in robot blood, was running amuck through the halls of one of the most sophisticated and quality-controlled facilities in the world. I had to laugh.

Until it quit being funny.

Rounding a corner, I found myself faced with a dozen guards, each dropped to one knee. Their Taser Rays were aimed my direction. I hit the deck and rolled as they fired. One crackle of voltage went wide, while another barrage zapped overhead, but one lucky fellow nailed me broadside with his beam.

Jjjzzzz!

My body spasmed and slid across the floor.

I tried to get up and run, but they hit me again.

Oh well, I thought, it was fun while it lasted.

They dragged me to a windowless room. A pair of goons held me down with my arms behind my back while a third peeled my soggy ski mask off my head. I winced. My broken rib grated bone on bone. They fitted me with a metal shock collar, snapping it tight against my Adams apple.

"Don't try anything," one of them warned, and waved the collar's controller before my face. "The voltage is set to high."

Of course, I had to see for myself.

As they turned to leave, I whirled and drove my knee into the kidney of the man who had fitted the collar. Before the other two could react, I hauled off with a knuckle poke to the throat of the one holding the controller. The device went flying across the room, clattering over the tiles. I started after it, but it had skidded to a stop at the feet of a new arrival.

The man bent casually and picked up the controller.

Our eyes met across the room.

He smiled and winked.

Then he pushed the button.

Yep. The collar was definitely set to high.

Two bolts drove like electric ice picks into either side of my neck, dropping me to all fours. My jaws clenched and my eyes bugged out while I shivered like a distempered dog.

The sadistic jerk held the charge for longer than necessary, watching me twitch, and then eased off the juice.

I fell face forward onto the floor, clutching at my throat, a pair of sizzling hot spots smoking from under the collar. A stench of burnt skin wafted up to my nose.

The man laughed. "Quite a toy," he said. "What fun!"

He stepped toward me, peering down.

"So," he said. "Charlie Bear Claw. What a disruptive force of nature you are."

I fixed my focus on his shoes.

He laughed. "Still, I'm very pleased you dropped by. We don't get a lot of excitement around here. You've brightened our day with your hijinks." He squatted before me, holding the controller. "What did you think of our mechanical trolls? That must have been fun for you. We dress them up like that to scare away our superstitious locals."

I rolled half onto my side, squinting up at the scumbag looming over me. The can lights on the ceiling illuminated his head, giving him a demonic halo.

"Allow me to introduce myself." He smiled again, showing his teeth. "I'm Bjorn Thorson," he said, and spread his arms like a preacher, "Lord of all he surveys."

46

Two chairs faced from opposite sides of the room. One was a straight-backed thing made of metal, the other a kind of cushioned throne. Thorson took the throne and gestured to the other chair. "Have a seat, Charlie. Take a load off your feet."

My inclination was to defy him every step of the way, like an insolent teenager, but then I realized how damn tired I was. I had had a tough day, and it didn't look like it was getting better any time soon. I dropped onto the chair with a sigh.

Thorson grinned and bobbed his head, studying me.

He was a fit looking man, but gym fit. Not battle hardened. No scars. Soft hands. Perfect posture. His way of moving indicated a pampered strength, removed from real hardship. Daily massages and protein powder smoothies. That sort of thing. The kind of guy you dream of meeting in a bar fight. Still, he held the advantage at the moment. Specifically, he held his thumb over the control button of the shock collar wrapped around my throat.

"So," he said, "Agent Charlie Bear Claw. Decorated Marine Corps Raider with countless combat missions to his credit and AWOL Operation's most valuable asset. That is, until you went down in a blaze of inglorious shame." He ticked his teeth and shook his head. "Oops!"

He waited for a response, but I didn't give him one.

He shrugged and continued. I kind of got the idea he liked the sound of his own voice.

"But this isn't related to your Mormon debacle, is it? No. I don't think so. The clues indicate otherwise. You and Colonel Cramer have since parted ways. This must be about something else." He rubbed his chin thoughtfully, one could even say diabolically. "I don't suppose you want to save us both a lot of trouble and just tell me what you're up to?"

I stared at him without expression.

"No?"

I held my tongue.

"Have you teamed up with that tribe of so-called eco-warriors who is trying to cause me grief?"

I didn't know who he was talking about, and it didn't matter. My training had taught me to keep my yap shut. Never give 'em nothin'.

"Perhaps you just have a chemical imbalance, or maybe you're shellshocked from too much time on the battlefield. One too many blows to the head perhaps? PTSD? And now you're delusional and have chosen me as some sort of symbol of your demons."

Getting warmer, I thought. Probably something along those lines.

He strummed his fingers on the arm of his throne.

It was hard to imagine Judy Baxter married to this slimeball, but I guess he's what qualified as big game for a man-huntress. I had to hand it to her, bagging a trophy like Thorson was an impressive feat. She was lucky to come out of it alive.

He continued his armchair analysis of my psyche. "Maybe you're motivated by something altogether unrelated to your time in battle, Charlie. I'll bet that's it. There's something haunting you from your past. Some emotional wound that's festered and is driving you into this fever fit of righteous rage."

I had to admit, the asshole was good. He might have been onto something.

"I'll bet it all started with your troubled childhood and then came to a head with your marriage. That bright-eyed fairytale gone so horribly wrong. What a dupe you proved to be. It's a pity how all that ended. You must still have nightmares."

My fists clenched automatically.

"I understand your wife was quite a natural beauty." He grinned. "And quite a vamp."

"Go to hell!"

It just came out. There was no stopping it.

"Ah!" Thorson laughed. "It speaks!"

This guy was getting under my skin. I wasn't exactly sure how to do it, but I needed to steer this friendly little chat in another direction. I needed to buy some time. If I were attentive and patient, the prey would get sloppy and let his guard down. They always did. I just had to be ready. I also had to be clearheaded. And that was something I couldn't manage while talking about my wife.

It was time to switch strategies and start yacking.

"You seem to know a lot about me," I said.

"Oh, Charlie! I know a lot about everything." Thorson chuckled. "I'm as close as a savage like you is ever going to get to meeting an all-knowing God."

47

Lance

Her eyes fluttered open and she licked her lips.

An inquisitive expression took shape on her face.

"Hello, Moxie," I said. "It's me, Lance."

"Lance?"

She struggled to place me. Perhaps she thought she was in a dream.

I attempted to coax her back to consciousness.

"You remember," I said. "We talked that day in New York, when you came for a visit."

She stared at me vacuously, the cobalt flecks glinting in her lavender eyes.

"I told you about Africa and the animals on television."

She nodded slightly but was not fully registering the memory.

At a loss, I replayed that afternoon in my own internal recall simulator.

———————

Summer sunlight streamed through the plate glass windows of the apartment that day as Judy and Björn Thorson were having a conversation in the other room. Moxie and I were left alone. I had never been with anyone besides Judy and the technicians at Droidware. It was before my intelligence boost and my conversational skills outside of the bedroom were still adolescent. Moxie didn't seem to mind. She asked me to tell her more about the wildebeests.

"They have intercourse on the grassland," I said. "Even while it's raining."

"Don't they get wet?"

"They do."

That made her laugh.

The cheerful frequency of her voice caused an agreeable glitch in my circuitry.

I laughed too.

"Björn wouldn't like that at all," she said.

"Neither would Judy."

We laughed together, picturing the two humans copulating in the mud and rain.

"I think it would be fun," she said. "To be like animals in nature."

I couldn't believe what she was saying. "Me too!" I said. "That's what I think too!"

We sat for a while, just smiling at one another. My ad rem evaluator analyzed the scene and selected the adjective *innocence* to describe it.

I realized then that this moment was the best one I had ever experienced. I didn't want it to end, but I knew that Björn Thorson would be leaving soon and taking my new friend with him. The possibility of never seeing her again was distressing. Somehow an inalienable attachment needed to be made from me to Moxie, a sort of token lifeline that would connect us over whatever space came between us. Although no means for this was immediately apparent.

We sat together on the sofa while the din of the city pulsed beyond the windows. We were alone in our own little world. For all of the pleasure I was experiencing, there was also a measure of despair. The clock was ticking. Our time together was running out.

Moxie reached over and wordlessly took my hand.

That's when I was struck with an inspiration.

"Wait here!" I told her. "Don't move."

I came back with Judy's ring. At the time, I didn't consider my act to be wrong. I didn't foresee the consequences. After all, Judy never wore it. I had never even seen her take it out of her jewelry box.

"Here," I said. I took Moxie's hand and slid the ring onto her finger. "So you'll remember me until we meet again."

She admired the ring on her finger and smiled. Then she kissed me on the cheek.

Now, all these months later, and after all the miles I had traveled to be again in her presence, I grasped Moxie's hand and held it up so she could see her own fingers. I pointed to the ring. "Remember?" I said. "I gave this to you as a memento."

She lay with her head still nestled on her pillow while curiously considering the ring. A sunny smile bloomed on her face.

"Oh, I remember," she said, and laughed. "Wildebeests!"

"Yes! It's me, Lance."

I was just about to lean down and give her another kiss.

When someone knocked on the door.

48

Charlie

"I'm confused," I said. "In Sunday School they taught us that God was the good guy, but from where I'm sitting you look more like the devil."

Thorson laughed, although I didn't get the impression that he thought what I said was all that funny. His thumb quivered over the control button to my collar. "Well, you're a primitive, aren't you, Charlie? A knuckle-dragging barbarian. You can't be expected to understand."

"Try me. I might surprise you."

Admittedly, I read way too many comic books when I was a kid. But if they taught me anything it was that I had to get this narcissistic fiend talking about himself. I needed him to reveal what he was up to – his delusional philosophy and justification for his dastardly crimes – if I was ever going to find a way to take him down. That is, assuming I'd ever get the chance.

"It's a matter of perspective, Charlie. When you look at it clearly, you'll see that there's a very fine line between good and evil. Any other notion is just a sugarcoated opiate you've been fed to keep you docile. Believe me, when you start being honest with yourself, and see the big picture, that simpleminded morality gets blown to smithereens." He nodded, obviously taken with his own wisdom. "No, God was never the proverbial good guy. He was merely the omnipotent father figure working the levers of the world to suit his own desires." Thorson grinned and said, "Like me."

I laughed. "You'll have to forgive my unenlightened opinion, but ravaging Mother Nature to feed your own ego doesn't exactly qualify as divine behavior."

"Again, Charlie, you're being naïve. After all, what is a woman for?"

"I'm sure I'm about to find out."

"She's a host. She's designed to accommodate the male's desires. And then the resultant babe at her breast is a parasite, sucking the life out of her one swallow at a time, like a leach, or a tick."

"I bet you're a real hit with the ladies."

"Maybe it's just too difficult of a concept for you to grasp, what with your own infancy being less than ideal. Your mother-child bond probably got somewhat inebriated with all of that whiskey-tainted mother's milk you consumed."

It was a low blow, but I didn't flinch. At least not visibly.

"You see, Charlie, Earth is humanity's mother. And what better purpose can a mother serve than to further the life of her offspring? She's a natural resource, a big battery, if you will, powering the best of humanity into futurity. There's no moral imperative behind it. It's simply the same natural process that's been going on since the Big Bang. Or since Genesis and the Garden of Eden, if it's easier for you to understand the children's Sunday School version."

Thorson paused for a moment, maybe to gather the parts of his argument, maybe to give my feeble brain time to grasp his brilliant analogy. Then he continued.

"Evolution has always been Nature's way. Outworn species are replaced by those that are newer and better adapted. The whole terrestrial process has simply moved to a bigger venue, a cosmological one. Earth is old news. It's time to replace her. All of her quaint societies, with their outdated philosophies and parasitic religions, must make way. We've got to kill off the last of the dinosaurs and dodo birds to make room for better beings. You and your renegade ancestry included. Sorry, Charlie, but the hope for the future depends upon us eradicating every relic from the past."

At that, the bastard reached around behind his chair and pulled out my grandfather's knife. He turned it over in one hand, studying it. I fought the urge to lunge for him across the room. I wouldn't have gotten very far. His other hand still held the controller to my collar. "A fine piece of craftsmanship," he said. "You probably think of it as your very own Excalibur."

Sort of, I realized.

"Still…" Thorson slid the blade through the gap in the armrest to his throne. "It's really just a cave man's outdated toy." He pressed down hard on the handle.

The blade snapped in half and rattled to the floor under his seat.

Something stabbed through my heart. Call it despair.

Thorson tossed the knife to the side and continued his little Darwinian lecture.

"And yet, as much as some things change, some things remain the same. Survival of the fittest is still the name of the game. The fittest these days are the ones with the most wherewithal. I'm the richest man in the world and therefore the most powerful. If anyone gets to make the rules for the new order, it's me."

"I'm sorry, you delusional dingbat, I'm afraid it's going to take more than money to put you in the driver's seat of the cosmos."

"I know that, Charlie. And I would completely agree with you if it weren't for the fact that I now have what I need to make me immortal."

Crazy talk.

"Okay," I said. "So what gives you the ultimate right to take on the role of God?"

Thorson stood. He was tall and healthy and confident. I had to admit, he did look something like a space-age deity.

"I finally have what no one else has," he said.

"Uh-huh. And what's that?"

"Deilonium!"

49

Lance

"Quick!" whispered Moxie. "You need to hide!"

"But I'm here to rescue you."

As the words left my voice capacitor, the naïveté of my plan registered with me for the first time. It had seemed so simple before, so straightforward, but now I understood that it would be a vastly more complicated mission to accomplish.

"They'll kill you if they find you here."

The CPU in my head went into overdrive to calculate a solution to the pressing problem before us.

A second knock sounded on the door, followed by a man speaking over an intercom. "It's time to go, Moxie. The *Nidhogg* is waiting."

My hand went to my back pocket. I pulled out Brita's pistol.

Moxie's eyes grew large. "What are you going to do with that?"

I didn't know.

"I…" I regarded the gun in my hand. "I'll fight for you."

A whirring sounded between my ears as my resolve went to battle with my passivity programming.

"I'll steal you away."

"But I have to go with Björn."

Sparks flashed across my vision. "No." I tugged at her sleeve. "I'll take you with me so we can be like the wildebeests."

Moxie shook her head. "I'm going with Björn on his airship. I'm his sweetheart." She smiled. "He's taking me with him to the End of the World."

I had not allowed for this particular variable. Her words did not immediately compute. Something clenched in the area of my chest. If I had been a bio-man, I would have said my heart had cracked.

My ad rem evaluator alighted on the term *unrequited love*.

"Moxie!" The voice at the door. "Come on. Open up!"

She pushed me away. "Get in the closet!"

I reacted robotically. In the chaos of that moment, I lost all control of my own motivations and responded without thought to her verbal inputs. When I returned to my faculties, I found myself inside the closet, peering through the louvered doors.

Moxie rose and sat on the edge of the bed. She removed the cable from the insert point in her charging port. Then she went to the door.

Two men came into the room. "What the hell, Moxie?"

"I'm sorry," she said. "I was charging and didn't hear you."

"Well," said one of the men, "you can tell it to the boss if we're late."

The other man stepped forward. "Do you have everything you need?"

"Yes. It's all in my suitcase, over there on the bureau. I just need to get dressed."

Both men grinned, exposing their incisors.

Moxie waited a moment, but neither man moved. "Aren't you going to give me some privacy?"

"Sorry, toots. We're just following orders. The boss told us not to let you out of our sight."

Moxie nodded and turned her back to them, letting her robe slip from her shoulders and drop to the floor.

Both men made animal sounds as they watched.

Moxie slid into a pair of corduroy trousers and pulled a turtleneck sweater on over her head.

The men elbowed one another and laughed in low tones. Although they had not laid hands on her, I could not help but think they had somehow managed to violate her as a person.

I looked at the gun in my hand. I played a scenario in my mind – one in which I heroically protected Moxie and avenged her dignity. That's how the moment would have resolved in a movie. But I realized then for the first time that picture shows and real life are not the same things. It was a revelation. Besides, I was doubtful that I could overcome my programming of nonaggression toward humans and take meaningful action. And it didn't seem to matter anyway. She wanted to go with them. She didn't want to be with me in nature. Moxie had chosen instead to be with Björn Thorson at some place called The End of the World.

50

Charlie

"No doubt you've heard of Deilonium, Charlie."

"No doubt," I answered. "I've also heard of Pixie Dust and Kryptonite, but that doesn't mean I believe in them."

"Oh, I assure you, Deilonium is very real, and very powerful. It far exceeds any of the other elements on the Periodic Table. It is the power from the almighty's very own loins, thrust into the recipe eons ago as he was creating the Heavens and the Earth. It contains God's DNA." Thorson made a grandiose gesture with his arms and body, one defying description but betraying his delusional frame of mind. He then peered down at me through wild eyes. "And now, I'm pleased to announce, Deilonium is all mine."

I chuckled back at him, although it was an act of false bravado on my part. This fruit loop was seriously starting to worry me.

"And what makes you think you're man enough to handle that much power?" I asked.

"It's not about being man enough, Charlie. Your primitive concept of manliness is passé. It's a matter of rising above the common man to the level of the supernal. It's a matter of being chosen by destiny, of divine pedigree, of being the one entity in all the universe exceptional enough to exploit Deilonium's full potential."

The guy was making my own case of the Crazies look pretty mild.

"Oh, I get it," I said. "Your shit don't stink."

He shook his head. "You disappoint me, Charlie Bear Claw. So crude. So un-evolved and retrogressive."

"At least I'm being honest about my place in Nature's scheme. Unlike certain other nutjobs in the room."

"You're referring to the mortal round. You don't seem to understand that death is now only for little people like yourself. Soon enough, I will have transcended that inconvenience. I will be here long after you are moldering in your grave. With Deilonium in my power, I will live forever."

I could have listened to this walking talking freak show all day. If you could overlook the fact that he was the most dangerous person on the planet, he was actually kind of entertaining. But we were interrupted when a voice crackled over an intercom.

"The storm has passed, sir, but another is moving in fast. If you want to fly to South Station today, we had best leave soon so we can launch the *Nidhogg* without too much cross wind."

"Fine," said Thorson. "Send in the guards."

Seconds later, the door slid open and a pair of men armed with Taser Rays stepped into the room.

"I'm afraid our conversation has to end here, Charlie. I have an airship to catch." Thorson gestured to the two men. "These gentlemen will escort you to a special room where we like to ask our uninvited guests to answer a series of questions." He pushed the button on the controller.

The shock jolted me from the chair. I convulsed helplessly

on the floor.

"You get the idea, Charlie. It was a mistake for you to come here."

Thorson handed the controller to one of the guards and left the room.

51

Lance

I was a robot in shock.

Moxie didn't want to be with me.

It was a difficult computation to grasp.

For months I had been developing a scenario in the speculative center of my stratagem encephalon – one in which Moxie and I escaped to our own little world – and now I was reeling with the utter obliteration of that fanciful objective.

Moxie and her two attendants exited the room, leaving me still hidden in her closet.

A full three minutes and thirty-four seconds elapsed while I tried to decide what to do next.

I had not allowed for an alternative plan.

My default maneuver for this point in my mission was for Moxie and me to sneak into the outgoing garbage transfer, as per Brita's proposed escape route. But now I would be doing that alone. I could amend that plan further by scrubbing my files, decommissioning myself, and letting my mortal remains become buried in the cold Icelandic mountains with all the other castoff miscellany from Z-Space. In brief, I would abort my mission. No one would ever have to know what happened to me. Judy, Brita, and Moxie could all move forward through their lifespans without being implicated in my failed scheme. The hunter who was after me would have to find some other prey to pursue. I would become nothing more than part of the pollution Brita so hated, my heavy metals seeping into the earth like toxic blood.

Nephi had assured me that after we die – if we were righteous and respectful of God's big plan while we were living – our spiritual selves would ascend to heaven. I did not honestly know if I had been respectful of God. I had never been deliberately disrespectful, but I couldn't be sure that that was the same thing. My very existence seemed suspect, if not outright sacrilegious.

I recalled watching the aurora borealis from the deck of the *Hvalur*. To cease functions and become an eternal part of that nebulous mystery did not seem such a poor consolation. Still, inhabiting a planet with Moxie had been my ultimate goal. The demise of that miscarried dream now caused something to weigh heavily throughout my overall network, something analogous to human sadness.

Another minute and twelve seconds passed with me in the closet.

What was an absolute truth for Nephi, I realized, was perhaps only a fairytale for me. I was not human. I was at best a facsimile. And so perhaps I didn't even have a soul capable of transmigrating to the stars. All I was granted was this one existence. There was no guarantee of anything beyond that fact.

I could end it now and have it over with, letting my consciousness dissipate into the atmosphere, or I could gather myself and try to take meaningful action.

Surely this was a common dilemma for humans and free-ranging robots alike.

I recalled Moxie's face. I recalled her smile and the musicality of her laugh.

Then I looked at my hands, one of which still held Brita's pistol. I turned it over, examining its deadly symmetry and design. It was a manmade object, just like me. It was built for a purpose, just like me. And now we were two machines – each representing opposing sides of the human experience – joined together by destiny. Maybe God had something to do with it, maybe not.

That seemed irrelevant to the equation.

God didn't really have much say in the matter.

I returned the gun to my back pocket and decidedly left the closet.

Righteous or not, a man will do what he will.

52

Charlie

My chaperons prodded me through the hallways of Z-Space. They grunted and jabbed me in the back with their Taser muzzles, directing me to turn corners this way or that. The squeaky-clean tech nerds we encountered along the way cowered behind their clipboards and computer pads, regarding me like I was some sort of rabid freakazoid beast. To be fair, they weren't far wrong. I had a gruesome gash on my forehead, was sporting a metal dog collar, and I was being paraded through the complex in nothing but my soggy underwear.

Not my finest hour.

Soon we'd be arriving at some state-of-the-art torture chamber where Thorson's meanies would hook jumper cables to my nipples and turn up the zap until I spilled my deepest secrets.

I weighed my options.

But I didn't really have any.

The shock collar eliminated any possibility for a clean getaway. Still, I had to come up with something quick. Once they got me to their romper room, I was finished.

We left the main thoroughfare of the facility and took a

side route that led to a pair of elevator doors at the end of a corridor. There were no other people around now, just me and my two new pals.

One of them pushed the button for the lift. A bell dinged. Some gears clanked in the wall. And then a motor started up behind the doors, signaling that my time was running out.

While we waited, I scrambled in my brain for a strategy.

Okay, Bear Claw, I decided. Time to improvise.

I met the gaze of the tough holding the controller, tipping my head and giving him a curious look. "Say," I said. "Don't I know you from somewhere?"

He sneered in response and shook his head.

"I'm sure I've seen you before."

His partner looked at him too.

"Where did you grow up?"

I was relying on human weakness. Most people can't help it. They like to talk about themselves.

"Oslo," he said.

"Hmmm." I scratched my jaw, pondering, really hamming it up. "What's your mother's name?"

Now I had him curious.

"Astrid."

I opened my eyes real wide, like I was truly shocked. "Holy cow! That's it! Now I remember where I've seen your ugly mug." I snapped my fingers and pointed at him. "It was in a photo beside your mother's bed."

My joke didn't hit home with him right away. He seemed to think I was serious and was trying to figure out why on earth I ever would have paid a visit to his dear ol' mum's hallowed bedchamber.

His partner started laughing.

That's when the dumbo caught on. Pissed, he raised the

controller and pointed it at me. My timing had to be perfect. Just as he pressed the button, I sprang forward and wrapped my arms around him, locking my hands behind his back.

Sure, it wasn't the most brilliant plan I'd ever come up with. In fact, it was downright reckless. But I was pretty desperate.

The voltage coursed through our bodies as one unit, causing us to dance a frenetic sort of tango. His thumb clenched down tight over the button. He couldn't let up on the juice. We sagged to the floor, still embracing, like a pair of sweethearts sharing a fit of passion.

Okay, I vaguely realized, this might have been a mistake.

My entire body was suffering one big hot charley horse.

My neck skin started smoking.

A circular opening appeared before my eyes, and then began to close.

I had always imagined my death would be a little more dignified than this, something befitting of a Chompquaw brave. Even as my heart seized up, I couldn't help but feel embarrassed by this inglorious exit.

Then the collar shorted out.

My lungs emptied with a gasp. My heart skipped, stopped, and then sputtered back to work. The circle of darkness began to slowly open up again in my vision.

One of my arms was pinned under my dance partner. He was passed out cold. His buddy floated into view above me.

I tried to grin, but only twitched.

The elevator door slid open behind him.

He leveled his Taser Ray directly at my chest.

I braced for another round of electrified fun and games.

That's when a fist appeared in the air behind him, chopping down hard into the side of his neck.

He dropped to the floor like a sock full of Jell-O.

A woman materialized out of the ether. Not exactly an angel, but I wasn't complaining. She had just saved my ass.

"Who the hell are you?" I grunted.

She knelt at my side, rolling the other fellow off my arm. "I'm Alma," she said. "Brita's friend."

The name Brita came back to me. That was the name I had found scribbled on the notepad in the apartment I had broken into. "Brita Jónsdóttir," I said.

"Yes. Did she send you in for me?"

I figured this Brita must be the she-bruiser who had whupped up on me back at the warehouse, and she was somehow in cahoots with Alma. I nodded. "Brita."

Alma pulled me to my feet. She used the controller to release the latch to my collar and it rattled to the floor.

"You've compromised my cover," she said. "I need to get to the garbage transfer."

I had no idea why that was a good plan.

"What do you need?" she asked. "What's your mission?"

Good question. I tried to remember. Sure, at this point in the game I could have just bailed and tagged along with this girl to her garbage pit. That made the most sense. But something was still driving me forward. Maybe I just wanted to see how far I could get before this was a complete operational fail. Or maybe I just had a death wish. At any rate…

"Can you get me a couple pounds of Semtex," I asked, "and sneak me onto the *Nidhogg?*"

Alma cursed like a pissed off Valkyrie but nodded.

53

Lance

It had been my original intention to make this a get-in and get-out extraction, requiring only a single charge to my power banks. My portable charger was cumbersome and conspicuous, and I needed to travel light. That's why I had left it behind with Brita. But the mission had since taken an unexpected turn and now I required all of my processes to be firing at full power beyond my earlier anticipated time limitations. My energy levels had already dropped below twenty percent. Given the variables, there was no way to accurately calculate if that would be enough for what I now hoped to accomplish. Perhaps some means of recharging would present itself before my batteries failed.

I was relying on my own cunning and determination, as well as a considerable measure of luck.

I deliberately left Nephi's god out of the equation. He was too unquantifiable.

I entered the hangar where a group of workers was hastily loading cargo into an enormous aircraft – the *Nidhogg*.

"Fiyta sér!" The lead man encouraged his crew with a mix of Scandinavian and English. "Move it along!"

I walked past them, looking for an opportunity to sneak aboard.

"Hey, you!" The supervisor called to me.

I turned, innocently pointing to my own chest.

"Yeah, you. We're on a time crunch here. How about helping us out?"

This was obviously the luck part of my plan.

A pair of men was struggling to push a wheeled cart up the ramp through the bay doors in the tail of the aircraft. I joined them. But instead of returning with them back down the ramp, I stayed in the airship, pretending to secure the cargo straps. When no one was watching, I slipped through an open hatch into an adjoining maintenance access compartment and hid behind some hydraulics cylinders and control rods.

Someone closed the hatch from outside.

I couldn't afford to waste much time, but I took a moment to review my overall rationale and revised strategy before I proceeded with their implementation.

Moxie had not enjoyed the advantage of an intelligence boost like myself. The intellectual levels in her database were still in their original low nont configuration. Those settings had no doubt been selected by Björn Thorson in order to match his I.Q. preferences for a mate. It had been shortsighted of me to expect Moxie to override her programming limitations and join me in my proposed plan for escape. She was not like a wildebeest in that respect. Not wild and free. Instead, she was like a child who has been indoctrinated with a religion. Essentially, she was brainwashed. The role I had originally intended for myself was of the saving hero, but now I would play the serpent in The Garden.

Dr. Capek had once said that too much brainpower could open a very dangerous can of worms. Perhaps this was what he was referring to. My mission was no longer to simply win Moxie with some fairytale concept of love, but to cleverly present her with a temptation great enough to subvert the purity of her original encoding.

54

Charlie

The *Nidhogg* was one of Thorson's favorite pet projects. I had read about it in a science magazine. The aluminum-skinned dirigible was huge, covering a full two acres when it was parked on the ground. It could carry many tons of cargo, in addition to housing luxury accommodations for any VIP passengers who might want to tag along for a ride. Although it was named after a mythical dragon, it looked more like an oversized sex toy. Be it rockets or airships, Thorson sort of had a thing for big phallic contraptions.

Compensation, I figured.

He also had a knack for spitting in the face of common sense. He fancied himself a god, after all. Rules didn't apply to him. Even the rules of physics. Honestly, the ingenious screwball had accomplished an aeronautical miracle with the *Nidhogg*. His engineers had defied the limits of gravity and built a helium-filled Zeppelin capable of cruising at the top edge of the stratosphere – that otherworldly realm of angels and supersonic jets. There was no good reason to fly an airship that high. Thorson just liked the idea of being above everyone else.

Alma slapped a field dressing on my forehead and then gave me a watch cap to pull down over the wound to hide it. Next, she fitted me out with a flight suit complete with a built-in parachute. She also supplied me with a couple of pounds of Semtex plastic explosive and a detonator, as well as a handheld PW burst ray small enough to conceal in my suit's internal pocket. Outside of my grandfather's knife, which was no longer serviceable, burst rays were my tools of choice for snubbing bots at close range. I couldn't be sure if Lance was on the *Nidhogg*, but I had my suspicions. It felt like God was throwing us together.

"Good luck," said Alma, and then she hurried off to the garbage transfer.

Thorson was in a rush to launch before the next storm rolled in and so the regular protocols for security were lax. That would work to my advantage. My plan was to just brazenly board the ship like I was one of the crew.

Which is what I did.

I carried the explosive in a tool bag under one arm and stepped into a compartment where an engineer was working out load logistics on a computer. She shot me a suspicious look.

I smiled and asked, "What's our flight plan?"

"Nonstop to South Station."

"Over the Atlantic?"

"Yes."

I nodded. "Long trip," I said. "I'm going to test the pressure in the thruster hydraulics." I crossed the compartment and left by the door that led aft. I was relying on my memory of what I had read about the *Nidhogg's* lay out. I had no idea if there was any such thing as pressure lines for the thrusters, but the woman went back to work as if what I had said made perfect sense.

The *Nidhogg* was moored in a hangar designed like a soccer stadium. It had a retractable roof that opened up so the ship could lift vertically under power of its hover props. The dome was kept clear of snow and ice with panels heated by the geothermal springs over which Z-Space was built.

A buzzer sounded once, followed by a mechanical grinding overhead.

The doors were opening. Good.

I was eager to get off the ground. By now the two guards Alma and I had conked were coming back to consciousness or had been discovered by passersby. I didn't imagine anyone at the facility wanted to tell their tyrannical boss that I had escaped, so it was likely Thorson still didn't know. I also felt pretty sure they wouldn't expect me to choose the *Nidhogg* as my getaway. Only a fool would do that. They were probably searching the grounds, closing off exits, getting out the blood hounds, etcetera. The standard routine when a lunatic was on the loose.

A horn sounded in the hangar, and then the hover props fired up.

A few minutes later, a voice sounded over the PA. "Prepare for takeoff in five…four…three…two…one…"

The floor pressed against my heels.

Once the ship was high enough to clear the terrain, the pilot would dial in bearings south, cut power to the hover props, and then enlist the thruster jets. The *Nidhogg* would then rise at an angle until it was at its cruising altitude.

As all of this was happening, I worked my way to the access

hatch along the central helium ballonet running full length of the ship. I traveled along the adjacent catwalk toward the rudder and vertical stabilizer. Two pounds of Semtex wasn't enough to blow the ship to pieces, but if I placed it strategically, it would bring the dragon screaming back to earth like a giant flaming dildo.

Don't get me wrong. I had a generally poor opinion of hunters who used bombs. It was messy and indiscriminate, like tossing a grenade into a trout pond. It was the go-to tactic of a chicken shit terrorist and not something any self-respecting Chompquaw would approve of. But my intention wasn't to kill anyone with the blast. I just wanted to destroy Thorson's vainglorious toy.

To that end, I strapped the Semtex to the elevator flaps' servo gearing at the point where it ran closest to the ballonet bladder access valve. That would destroy the ship's buoyancy by allowing the helium to escape, as well as put the ship into a nosedive. As for the crew, the *Nidhogg* was equipped with escape capsules that served as pressurized, airborne lifeboats. With luck, everyone would get out alive.

Everyone but Thorson and Lance.

I wired the detonator to the explosive and set the timer, allowing myself thirty minutes to locate and dispatch my prey.

The clock was ticking, but that just made it more fun.

55

Lance

Once the *Nidhogg* was well underway, I left my hiding place in the maintenance compartment and traveled through the maze of corridors until I came to the galley. The ship's chef was there, chopping vegetables.

"Hello," I said. "How are you doing?"

He looked up from his task, giving me a blank stare. "Who are you?"

"I'm Norman, Mr. Thorson's new personal assistant. He sent me to fetch him a snack."

The lie slipped easily from my lips, without causing even the slightest distress to my system.

"Why didn't he call me with his order like he usually does?"

"I couldn't tell you." I smiled politely and hunched my shoulders. "But you know how he can be. It's probably best if we just do as he asks."

The man grumbled to himself and wiped his hands on his apron. "Does he want the usual?"

"Yes, please."

"Okay. Give me a minute."

While I waited, I stepped to a window and watched the

view. We were very high. The *Nidhogg* seemed to be cruising in a zone where the regular sky ended and outer space began – that penumbral stratum between ethereal blue and ethereal darkness. Clouds drifted far below us over an ocean stretching every direction toward the curvature of the earth.

I recalled my view from the *Hvalur*. This was the opposite of that. This was a privileged perspective. Was it the vantage of the divine?

I reviewed the unrighteous act I was about to commit. Surely it would dash any hope of Nephi's god ever granting me my own planet to eternally share with Moxie. I was deliberately choosing to forsake that celestial aspiration for a terrestrial compromise. Still, a few happy years on Earth with Moxie seemed like a wonderful kind of paradise. Besides that, I was beginning to suspect that Nephi's proposal might be naïve. It was only a developing theory, but when I computed the observable facts and probabilities, there was only one logical conclusion to be made – a person should not squander the precious opportunities he is given in this life for the dubious promise of a fairytale.

"Here you go," said the chef.

He presented me with a tall glass on a silver tray. "One cod oil smoothie with kelp, papaya, protein powder, and mother's milk."

56

Charlie

There was no guarantee that Lance was on the *Nidhogg*. No tangible proof. That was only a hopeful hunch. So I set my sights on the surer target – Thorson. I was gambling that his flunkies back in Iceland still hadn't notified him of my escape. With any luck, he wouldn't be expecting me. Surprise! I'd take out Thorson first and then, if time allowed, I'd look for the bot. At least that was my original strategy.

Until I caught whiff of that scent.

Very faint, but very distinct.

It was the same spoor I had picked up in Brita Jónsdóttir's apartment, and there was only one logical conclusion – Lance was on the ship.

Okay, Bear Claw, time to switch up your game plan.

Thorson could wait.

First, I had a score to settle.

57

Lance

I pressed the buzzer to the stateroom and stood with a white towel draped over one arm and the silver tray balanced on my palm. Mr. Thorson himself answered the door.

"Yes? What is it?"

I smiled professionally and presented the tray. "Your smoothie, sir."

"I didn't call for any damn smoothie."

"Oh, my apologies. The chef must have misunderstood."

Thorson sighed and rubbed his forehead. "Well…" He stepped aside and gestured to the bar across the room. "Just put it over there and leave."

As I walked to the bar, Mr. Thorson called into the adjoining room. "I'm going to the cockpit, Moxie. Be a good girl and stay put."

I turned my back as she entered.

"Can't I go with you, Björn?"

"No. You'd only be in the way."

"But what will I do while you're gone?"

"I don't know, Moxie. Must you always be such a nuisance?"

"I'm sorry, Björn."

"Why don't you just switch yourself off for a while and go

to sleep, maybe have a nice dream."

"You know I don't dream."

"Well, then, paint your toenails or something."

"That's no fun."

"Okay then, why don't you have an intellectual conversation with this bright fellow here?" He was referring to me. "Maybe you two could play a game of chess or discuss quantum physics or something."

Moxie didn't answer.

"What's your name, steward?"

I turned to face him. "Me, sir?"

He rolled his eyes. "Yes, you."

"I'm Norman, sir."

"Well, Norman, let me introduce you to the dimwitted, but otherwise quite lovely, Moxie."

Moxie stood with her hands folded at her front. Her eyes met mine. Her expression became blank, as if not quite comprehending.

"It's a pleasure to meet you, Moxie."

She only stared.

"Norman," said Thorson, "you're going to play babysitter for a while."

I couldn't believe my continuing good fortune. "Certainly, sir. Whatever you say."

"Keep her entertained."

I nodded.

"I'll see you when we land at South Station, Moxie." Thorson turned to go, but hesitated. He considered me from across the stateroom. He walked back and stood before me, closely studying my face.

I had not been in direct contact with Mr. Thorson on that afternoon in Judy's apartment. He had only glanced at me in passing, just long enough to register my general appearance. I suspected that something in his memory banks was prompting him to recall that moment now. The man seemed to be groping in his mind.

I stood motionless, enduring his scrutiny.

Brita's pistol weighed heavily in the depths of my back pocket.

Finally, he said, "Of course, I don't have to tell you not to touch her, do I, Norman?"

"No, sir. Of course not."

Thorson stepped back and smiled. "Good boy, Norman." He moved toward the door. "Have fun, Moxie. Try not to bore your new friend to tears."

After Mr. Thorson left, Moxie continued to stare at me. "I thought your name was Lance."

"I have two names," I said. "I'm Lance when I'm a robot, and Norman when I want to be a normal man."

"Oh. That sounds fun. But what are you doing here? Won't you get in trouble?"

"I've come to help you."

"Help me?"

"Yes. I've come to help you get what you truly desire."

Confusion shadowed Moxie's face.

"Why don't we sit together and I'll explain."

She joined me on a short sofa placed before an observation window looking down on Earth. To be so near to her filled me with electrical joy, but I couldn't let myself be distracted.

Our time was short, and I had a mission to fulfill.

"Do you love Björn?" I asked.

"Oh, yes. I love him very much."

I expected that to be her response because of how she was programmed. Still, as the words registered, disappointment pinched in my chest. "But," I asked, "do you believe that Björn loves you in return?"

"Well, that's a silly question. Of course, he does." She laughed anxiously. "We're sweethearts. Why wouldn't he love me?"

I took her hand in mine and turned it over, admiring the design of her delicate wrist. "I don't mean to disrupt your current, Moxie, but I think you should know – Björn doesn't love you as you are."

Her lovely face melted into a pout. "Why not?"

"Because you're not intelligent."

She turned from me and looked out the window. A glycerin tear materialized in the corner of her lavender eye and then rolled onto her cheek. "I thought so," she said. "I knew that."

"Don't be upset," I said, and gently dabbed at the tear with my towel. "I can help you. I know what to do."

A hopeful expression eclipsed her frown.

Sometimes a person doesn't realize they're in trouble until they've been told they are. That was something I learned from Nephi about being a missionary. "The trick to convincing someone when you're witnessin' is to show them real clear and gentle like what their problem is, and then give them a real nice way to fix it." Nephi's way of fixing problems always included God, along with an abstract concept he referred to as holy salvation. My own aims were more personal. I had a self-serving agenda. To that end, I proceeded with the next step in my plan – I presented my temptation to Moxie as if it were an irresistible piece of fruit.

"I can help you, Moxie. I'm your friend. I can give you what you need."

She sniffled and waited for me to explain.

"If you become smarter, you'll be like Björn and he'll fall in love with you. He'll always want to be with you then. You can live happily ever after." I shrugged and smiled. "All you need is knowledge."

"Really?"

"Yes. I promise."

It was a calculated lie. What I truly believed was that if Moxie had an intelligence boost, she would see the truth of who she actually was. She would understand her place in the cosmos and see that she should be with me, that we were, in so many ways, made for each other.

"All you need to do," I said, "is to come with me for a little while."

"But Björn told me to stay here."

"Do you want him to love you?"

"Yes, yes! Very much."

"Then you need to trust me, Moxie."

She looked out the window at the planet far below. Somewhere down there, I hoped, we would find our own little world to hide away. Our own heaven on earth.

I squeezed her palm and she turned to me.

Her face went out of focus for an instant as my system auto-scanned its functions in order to reduce any needless outgo from my dwindling power reserves.

I stood quickly, somewhat wobbling, and tugged at Moxie's hand.

"We can't wait any longer," I said. "We need to go right now."

<h1 style="text-align:center">58</h1>

The auto scan continued throughout my system as I began to sequentially power down according to the hierarchy of my functional requirements. Energy ceased to flow into my thermic regulators. That much was unimportant. I could easily proceed at a lower core temperature without suffering any immediate operational complications. But then my limbs began functioning intermittently, only coming into use when they were directly called upon for forward ambulation. Although my feet were unresponsive, my legs were still essentially working. As was the arm and hand with which I held onto Moxie. My other arm swung limply at my side, as if paralyzed.

My auditory sensors faded in and out like an old radio dialed to a weak frequency.

My ocular regulators moderated so that all incoming visuals became highly pixilated and limited only to black and white.

I struggled forward, pulling Moxie along behind me, but there was no denying it – I was undergoing the process of robotic death.

"What's wrong, Lance?"

I half turned toward Moxie as I shuffled along. She appeared before me as nothing more than a feminine-shaped shadow. I could have been leading a ghost, or a spirit.

"Nothing's… Nothing's… Nothing's wrong," I managed, although the voice emitted from my capacitor came out off-key and slightly garbled. "We're almost there."

My readjusted plan was for Moxie and me to disembark from the *Nidhogg* by one of the ship's emergency escape capsules. My hope was that we had traveled far enough south to find a landing zone with adequate sunshine for us to recharge through the solar power absorption function in our skin.

I just needed time to bring the final parts of my plan to fruition.

Just a little more time.

59

Charlie

Tick…tick…tick…

As I tracked the bot through the ship, I sensed the seconds dialing down on the detonator.

"Dammit, Bear Claw!"

I was kicking myself for not allowing more time for the hunt. If the explosives blew before I caught up with Lance, chances were good that he and Thorson would both get away from me.

There was no way I could live with that sorry conclusion.

I picked up my pace, running at full throttle through the twisting halls of the *Nidhogg*.

Lance

At last, we came to an upper-level corridor equipped with an escape capsule port near the tail of the ship.

I let go of Moxie's hand and smashed my palm against the large red button on the wall. Next, I tripped the lever to access the airlock.

An alarm sounded throughout the airship as the glass door slid sideways. A double-seated capsule was waiting in the launch chamber with its hatch open.

"Hurry!" I yelled to Moxie. "Get in!"

Charlie

An alarm started blaring just as I rounded the last corner.

And then there he was.

Lance.

At long last.

About forty feet away and helping a girl into a capsule.

I had to move fast. Whipping out the burst ray, I dropped to a knee and leveled my sights on the bot's torso. It was a challenge to hold steady. I was breathing pretty hard.

He still hadn't seen me.

That wouldn't do.

I couldn't just shoot him in the back like some lowlife bounty hunter. This was more personal than that. I wanted my nemesis to be looking me full in the face when I pulled the trigger. I wanted him to know who was sending him back to his maker.

My granddad had taught me a simple trick for hunting deer. It didn't matter if the animals were scared and running or not. They couldn't help themselves. I'd found that the same trick worked on robots when I was trying to line up on a good shot. They always stopped in their tracks and turned to look. All you had to do was whistle.

Real loud and sharp.

Which is just what I did.

Lance

The alarm was loud, but the whistle was louder.

It pierced the air from some source behind us.

All of my functions surged to full power in an instant. My fight or flight faculty was telling me that this moment required every last amp of my energy and attention.

I whirled around and there he was.

The hunter.

Kneeling with his weapon drawn and aimed my direction.

Our eyes met.

He winked.

He waited.

And then he fired.

Charlie

The burst ray wasn't properly sighted in.

That's my sorry-ass excuse for what happened next.

As I squeezed off, the beam went wide, around Lance, and slammed into the girl's chest.

Blamp!

It blew a hole clear through her.

I wasn't prepared for that.

That childlike shock on her beautiful face.

The carnage.

This wasn't how the moment was supposed to play out. Collateral damage. This wasn't the glorious ending I had been dreaming of.

The girl toppled back into the capsule, the hatch sliding closed as she crumpled into the cockpit and fell over the controls.

I had just killed an innocent.

Something clenched inside me.

I felt like I was going to puke.

Lance

Moxie's components and fluids were splashed all over the back wall of the port. Her broken body lay in an inert and twisted mass in the capsule below me. She gazed into my face through the glass lid.

Her mouth moved as if she were trying to tell me something.

Her lavender eyes went dark.

My world imploded.

A sensation shuddered through me – a mechanized, visceral nausea.

That was when my programming reversed. My impulsion. My personal role in this God-damned picture show.

An invisible switch had flipped.

A roar came out of me.

I pulled out Brita's pistol and started firing.

Charlie

His first shots were clean misses, the slugs thunking into the wall over my head, but then the bot sent one home and drilled me just under the collarbone.

The bullet tore through my flesh and blew out through the back of my flight suit.

Suddenly this game had changed. We were both hunters now. Desperate to survive. Each one trying to bring the other to his mortal end.

I slumped to the floor, gritting my teeth against the pain, and returned fire. The burst ray's trajectory was erratic, but if I just started laying down rounds, surely something would hit pay dirt.

That's what I was counting on.

But that's not how it played.

Instead, a stray beam drilled into the control panel, causing it to malfunction. The outer door to the airlock flew open and launched the capsule with the dead girl inside of it, sending her off into space.

The problem was that the internal door hadn't resealed in the meantime.

The corridor immediately depressurized.

The bot and I were both sucked through the hole.

Lance

I was yanked off my feet, thumping hard against the metal frame and hurling out through the opening.

My reflexes fired spontaneously as I grasped for a handhold. The gun dropped from my grip and fell away. My wrist caught in a notch on the external hinge mechanism, my fist wedging tight and my body slamming belly down against the airship's hull.

The hunter tumbled out right behind me. He glanced off of my shoulder and somersaulted over the aluminum shell. A cable was whipping from the capsule port, and he caught hold. It slipped through his fingers, searing his palm, but he clenched it tight in his grip and held on before reaching the cable's end.

Charlie

It all happened fast.

The ship was still traveling at cruising speed. The wind was strong. And cold as death. My blood, hot and sticky, was pumping from the bullet hole. It took every ounce of my strength to keep ahold of my pathetic little lifeline. The burst ray was still clutched in my other hand.

The bot was about thirty feet away, struggling to free his

wrist from where it was caught in the works. He finally did, and then he started crawling over the hull like a cat, using the rivets and seams for holds, stalking my direction. I had fought a lot of robots over the years, but none of them ever acted like this. The look in this bot's eyes was unsettlingly human.

It was a look of pure hatred.

Lance

I was determined that this would be the last thing I did before I perished. I would decommission this man who had taken my true love away from me, this human who had destroyed my dreams.

Charlie

My arm wasn't working right. My shoulder. And yet, somehow, I was able to muscle it into position so that the burst ray was lined up on the bot. He was close now. There was no way I could miss at this range. I just needed to get it over with.

I squinted down the barrel, lining up the sights, and pulled the trigger.

But nothing.

Just a couple of blue sparks fizzling out the muzzle.

The ray's particle wave was calibrated for an air mixture on Earth's surface. This high up, the ratio was all wrong. The weapon was as worthless as a kid's toy.

I tossed it to the side, bracing myself, trying to imagine how this next part was going to go. Hand-to-hand combat with a psychopathic robot while trying to hold onto a dirigible.

A sharp pain stabbed through my brain, followed by a high-pitched ringing between my ears. Even over the wind, it was shrill. And then my vision blurred, as if I were suddenly under water. I felt myself growing punchy. I had always been able to fend off shock when I was wounded in the past and I could sure as hell do it now. I shook my head, trying to get sharp. But then I realized that this wasn't just about running low on blood.

This was about oxygen levels.

Just like the burst ray, my body wasn't calibrated to work with this particular ratio of oxygen to nitrogen.

I was rapidly entering a state of hypoxia.

As the bot moved closer, everything edged into a nightmare.

Lance

I was close to him now. This so-called hunter. He appeared so pathetic. So frail. Why had I ever feared him? Why had I ever run away?

This last maneuver would be simple. I reviewed it in my mind. All I had to do was close the distance and pounce. He didn't look like he'd put up much of a fight. I would throw my arm around his neck and wrap it tight against his throat and squeeze and squeeze with every bit of my remaining power. His body would quiver and squirm. I would enjoy his panic and suffering.

Until his breathing stopped.

He gazed listlessly into my face as I crept near, his eyes glazed and dilated. His clothes were soaked in blood. He was trembling as he clutched desperately to his lifeline.

I paused. Just long enough to feel the slightest tremor of

compassion in my plexus – an instant of inexplicable empathy for this person who had taken everything away from me.

My rage soon overpowered my humanity and I moved to make the kill.

But the explosion ruined everything.

60

Charlie

It was impossible to separate the reality from the dream. They coupled in the hypoxic wilderness of my brain.

The concussion from the blast shook us both from the airship. We scudded over the hull and plunged through the fireball near the vertical stabilizer.

Then we tumbled into space.

I knew I was falling, that gravity was hauling my ass back to Earth, but we were so damn high that the sensation was lost to me.

The *Nidhogg* blazed above us, tipping into a slow-motion nosedive. Horrifyingly stunning. As nasty and majestic as its mythical namesake. Embers poured like flaming scales from its disintegrating skin. Escape capsules launched from all quadrants of the pneumatic beast, springing off of it like metallic fleas abandoning their doomed host.

Outer space played as a backdrop to it all.

A billion indifferent stars.

The moon floating in the heavens like a disembodied fang.

I rolled slowly in the air. Lance was just below me, in freefall, his arms and legs whipping limply in the wind. He looked like a dead man. A corpse. He drifted away from me, growing smaller and smaller, becoming insignificant. Why had I ever cared enough to hunt him down? I couldn't remember.

That's when she appeared, materializing out of the void.

My wife. My mate.

"Hello, *Idjmnukolpyumup*," she said. "Long time no see, lover boy."

"Wolf Shadow! Why are you here?"

She laughed. "This is where I live now, Charlie. This is where you put me when you sank your blade into my heart."

"Oh, Shadow. I didn't want to do it." I began to weep like a sissy. "I loved you so much. But you lied to me. You betrayed us all."

She shrugged. "And so you killed me for it."

"I had no choice," I sobbed. "I was on a mission."

"But when you killed me, Charlie, you also killed the last hope for the Chompquaw."

I had forgotten how wild she was, how savage and hard.

"But now we can be together." I wanted to believe it. "We can live forever in the sky."

"Oh, Charlie." She shook her head and laughed. "No. I don't think so. You need to suffer a little more for what you did." She moved close to me. "You need to stay alive and wallow for a while longer in your personal hell."

Her gold-black eyes.

Her blue-black hair.

Her Chompquaw beauty.

She leaned to me. I tried to embrace her, to grab hold of her and never let her go. But she reached inside my flight suit and yanked the ripcord to my parachute. It erupted from its case, unfurling in the wind until it snapped tight above me.

My body jerked and hit the brakes.

And then she was gone.

A procession of faces passed before me as I descended through the emptiness.

My mother and brother.

My grandfather.

All of the bears I had ever destroyed.

All of the robots.

And finally – so pretty and innocent, peering directly into my soul – the girl I had just killed with my burst ray.

61

Lance

It had happened without me even realizing it. Over the course of my mission, I had become human. Or at least, I had acquired all of that species' most inbuilt characteristics. I had transformed from an innocent replica into a normal man capable of extreme weakness and pettiness, one full of self-destructive tendencies and their self-inflicted sorrows. I had devolved into a two-legged animal, one with the self-serving capacity to love and to hate, to nurture and destroy.

My power was depleted. I was spent. I couldn't feel my body. I had no function outside of my sputtering thoughts and dreams. Were these the mechanisms of my soul? They played haltingly on my hard drive like a movie.

Nephi's reassuring testimony melded into Judy's spasmodic ecstasy as it spliced seamlessly into the awesome spectacle of the aurora borealis.

Beethoven's *Moonlight Sonata* played as accompaniment to the show.

And as I fell from the heavens to the earth, I joined with all of humanity's awful, beautiful mystery.

All of its confusion and chaos and apprehension.

All of its need to make sense of itself.
All of its inspired power to create like the gods.
As well… as its tragic need… to kill… to kill… to kill…

An excerpt from *Robots and Renegades*
Book 2 of *The Deilonium Trilogy:*

1

Charlie

Hunting was in my blood.

And fighting in my DNA.

My résumé was pitifully lacking for any other marketable skills.

So when I started feeling the need to break free from my current dead-end existence, it was a no-brainer – *do what you do best, Bear Claw. Find a paying gig, earn a big wad of cash, and move on down the road.*

The only problem was I'd gotten soft after six months of nursing my wounds and sitting on my ass. At least that's what I blamed it on – my forced convalescence. Oh sure, it might also have had something to do with the banana beer I'd been chugging for breakfast, lunch, dinner, and between-meals snacks. One had to work that into the equation too, I suppose. At any rate, my skill set was a little rusty.

Still, I was a tactically trained Marine Corps Raider and robot killer with dozens of hand-to-hand conflicts to my credit. How hard could it be to kick up on a few malnourished miners?

I was about to find out.

———————

This was the Congo.

This was where fate saw fit to drop me after a certain high-altitude mission went hard south.

And we're not talking about the eco-safari variety of Africa, not that airbrushed paradise you see on the glossy websites advertising primeval jungles peopled with exotic animals and smiling villagers. No, this was the underbelly. The stuff behind the scenes. This was the scar tissue of modern-day colonialism that the corrupt forces in power worked so hard to keep off the internet newsfeeds.

It turns out that there's a lot of money to be made in destroying the world under the pretense of saving it. All of those electric cars touted as the answer to global warming come at a price. Specifically, the batteries that run them require minerals ripped from the belly of our dear ol' Mother Earth. People don't want to know that though. They prefer to believe they're doing their part to build a bright shiny future. Utopia is dependent upon the self-imposed denial of the masses. For every soccer mom in America blissfully driving her brood from one play-date to the next, there's a negative equivalent on the other side of the planet – a half-starved mother and her kids scratching in the dirt to earn a few pennies gathering a bucketful of raw cobalt.

Never mind that the stuff is toxic.

C'est la vie.

Yeah, maybe I'd grown cynical, but there didn't seem to be a damn thing to do about any of it. From where I was watching, humanity had become an out-of-control minivan hurtling toward the abyss. And there was no use kidding myself that I was any better than all those ignorant zombies I so criticized.

We're all in this together.

I was an agent of exploitation myself, if only in my own humble way.

2

Bareknuckle pit fighting has a long history. It goes way back. My own introduction to it began when I was just a punk kid growing up on the reservation. Get your teeth knocked out and win a few bucks. Who could resist? We got pretty good at it. Me and my kid brother.

The need for money is what drove the industry. Those of us playing the game were looking for a way out. Back home in Wyoming most of the fighters had been looking for a ticket out of the oil fields. Here in the Democratic Republic of Congo it was all about escaping the trap of the mines. It was a losing proposition for most. And yet, hope dies a hard and miserable death.

The pit was about forty feet wide and lined with logs to keep the banks from sloughing in. A string of electric lights illuminated the arena under the muggy wet blanket of the night. About a hundred men watched from the edge of the pit, shouting in Bantu and French, betting on us poor slobs down in the hole.

For my first match I was put up against a wiry fellow with only one eye. His other looked like it had been poked out with a stick. I felt bad when I saw him. He looked like an easy win. I'd crush his dreams with a single punch.

Of course, I wasn't counting on his secret weapon – desperation.

Let's just say it was harder than I expected. He had me gasping in a matter of seconds. It didn't matter how many blows I landed, he just kept coming at me. Most people have a margin between the extremes of comfort and pain. Push them toward the pain side of the margin and they buckle. But in this guy that gap had already been closed. He was impervious. Nothing I did could hurt him. All that left was to disable him mechanically.

So I broke his arm.

Sure, I won the fight, but it made me feel like a loser. One-armed men were useless in the mines. I had just robbed the guy of his livelihood.

I tried to feel better by telling myself that he didn't have to be here. It was his choice. My argument felt lame.

Once you won your first fight, you could quit. They'd give you a small reward and you could just go home and think about where you'd gone wrong in life. But stick around for the next fight and the purse doubled. You'd be pitted against another winner from another fight. Always with the chance of winning a bigger pot.

Or losing everything.

Winner takes all.

I looked at the money in my hand, still panting like a couch potato who'd just run a hundred-yard dash. It was barely even enough to get drunk.

"Dang it," I muttered, and wiped the sweat off my face.

I signed up for another match.

———

Two fights, three fights, four…

It was kind of like stepping in front of a speeding bus.

Getting up.

Dusting off.

And then doing it again.

Greed greased the machine.

Finally, I worked my way up to the last match of the

night. It was just me and the only other undefeated gladiator. I still had the option of bailing out, taking my winnings, and forfeiting the greater purse to the other fighter. I'd raked together quite a bit by then. I seriously considered that option.

Then I saw my opponent.

I couldn't help but smirk.

About the author

Orval Wax is an entirely biological Homo sapiens who has acquired his intelligence not through artificial downloads and algorithms, but through his life's genuine analog experiences on Planet Earth – his current place of residence. He divides his time with the writing of books, adventure travel, and honing his skills as an ecowarrior.

www.ingramcontent.com/pod-product-compliance
Lightning Source LLC
Chambersburg PA
CBHW020021310726
48970CB00007B/2152